Blame It On Texas

Enjoy the romance!
Roni Denholtz

RONI
DENHOLTZ

Tyler was one appealing male!

She fought the thought, resisting his compelling presence.

"Comfortable?" he whispered, his voice a husky timbre.

"Uhm—yes." She didn't like the fact that she sounded like a schoolgirl.

Another good-looking cowboy, flirting with her. Normally she laughed it off and moved away.

But *I'm stuck in the saddle with you*, she thought.

Something tightened inside her at the thought, almost as if… as if she was *glad* to be stuck with him.

Dedication

For My Avalon "Sisters"--
My fellow authors who wrote for Avalon Books
during the same time I did.
You are a wonderful group of friends and writers,
some of the most positive people I know.
There are too many of you to name here, so let me just
say I value our friendships so much!
And to my first editor, Erin Cartwright Niumata.

Acknowlegments

A big thank you to Carolyn Brown for inviting me to participate in the world of the Palo Duro Canyon;

to Holly Jacobs for allowing Sunny and Josh to make a guest appearance;

and to Judi Fennell, editor/formatter/cover designer extraordinaire!

ALSO BY RONI DENHOLTZ

Setting the Stage for Love
Borrowing the Bride
A Taste of Romance
Salsa with Me
Marquis in a Minute
Negotiating Love
Somebody to Love
Lights of Love

CHAPTER I

"Wow! Here comes one hot cowboy!"

RaeAnne Tilton seconded her friend Kristy's assessment of the guy headed their way. Six feet of a lean, hard build with wavy black hair and dark chocolate eyes, he was as gorgeous a specimen of masculinity as the stallion beside him.

Wow.

"Is *he* the one I'm riding with? Lucky me." The model beside RaeAnne added a little "yee-haw" to the end of her awed comment.

It had to take a lot to get that kind of reaction from Selena, the top model in Houston, especially since she'd been grouchy all morning, but this guy—Tyler—had done it just by showing up.

"I believe he is," RaeAnne replied with an inner sigh. Hopefully Selena's attitude would be more positive now. The model had been getting on everyone's nerves all morning, from Dan the photographer, to Kristy and Sean, his assistants, and even her. RaeAnne's editor had been thrilled to get the top model for their photos. But so far RaeAnne was finding time spent with Selena far from thrilling.

"He's yummy." Selena moved forward, shaking

1

her long white-blonde hair down her willowy body. "Hi, cowboy. We're going to be sitting together for some photos," she drawled, smiling and batting her eyelashes.

"So I hear." But he didn't smile back.

The wind gusted, swirling some of the red dirt the area was so prone to around them, reminding RaeAnne of her childhood, the intense summer heat, the blazing sun, the dry air against her skin.

Or maybe that was the effect he had on her.

She shook her head and pushed back a swath of thick hair, then reached for her red cap. She didn't have time to notice how hot Tyler was—because she and everyone else were hot too. In a totally different way, but one that was way more pressing. They needed to get this photo shoot over with.

As if reading her mind, Selena complained, "I should be allowed to wear a hat."

"Now, Selena," RaeAnne said in a calm tone, "you know we spoke about this yesterday. The readers of *Texas Trails Magazine* will want to see your beautiful face in the photos." She swallowed, hating that she needed to use flattery to get the model in a good mood.

"They can still see my face with a hat on," Selena responded, frowning.

RaeAnne sighed. Their editor, Penny, had picked Selena from dozens of models because she thought she'd look good in these photos of Palo Duro. It was part of their article for next summer on little-known places to visit in Texas.

There had been a glitch, though. Just after Selena had signed the contract to do this photo shoot, she'd been offered a modeling job for another, larger Texas magazine, right in Houston itself. Her agent had tried to get her out of the contract with *Texas Trails* but Penny had been firm. She was committed to them for this time frame. And Selena had been decidedly upset that she couldn't take the other job, according to her agent.

And since this article was RaeAnne's idea— approved by Penny, of course—she was especially interested in seeing everything go well. They had three other towns lined up, too, but this, the first one to be written about and photographed, would probably be the most challenging.

She pasted a smile on her face.

And she had a special interest in this area. Not just because she was born and lived her first five years here—but because it was going to be part of her secret book project.

"It's so hot," Selena was muttering now.

RaeAnne snapped back to the present. The wind had died down as abruptly as it had started, and the sun beating down on them was quickly raising the temperature. She reached for her bottled water and took a swig. "Want more water?" she asked the model, then gulped some down.

"No." Selena pouted.

"Well, let's get moving," Dan, the main photographer, said. "I'm set up now. Let's take these shots before it gets hotter. Selena," he continued, putting his tripod down, "I want you on that horse, and then Tyler, you climb on behind Selena."

Tyler shook Selena's hand. "Tyler Quimby." His Texas drawl was sexy as all get-out.

Selena shook it, staring up at Tyler.

3

Tyler shook hands with Dan, Kristy, and Sean. Then he turned to RaeAnne.

The guy was way too good looking for her own good. She did *not* want to notice him. Didn't want to feel this way. She didn't need this sort of complication in her life. Not now.

But she couldn't refuse to shake his hand. That'd be unprofessional—and a dead giveaway that she was having anything but professional thoughts about him. "RaeAnne Tilton." she held out her hand, hoping her voice sounded as smooth as she intended. "Assistant editor."

"Pleased to meet you, ma'am." He tipped his hat and shook her hand.

Whoa. Tingles shot from her hand, all the way up to her head—and down to other more *interesting* areas.

She swallowed again, her throat suddenly as dry as the dust around them.

Oh my gosh. She hadn't felt that kind of sudden zing—sexual awareness—whatever it was, in years. RaeAnne looked at Tyler and saw an answering spark in his eyes. Oh no. It must be—it had to be—a figment of her imagination.

The last thing she needed was another instant attraction to a handsome cowboy. That hadn't worked out so well for her in the past.

"Okay, get on up behind Selena," Dan instructed, breaking the charged silence that RaeAnne was all too aware of.

Tyler headed toward the horse, but his gaze remained on RaeAnne longer than necessary.

"What was that all about?" Kristy tapped her on the shoulder.

RaeAnne dragged her eyes off Tyler's, um, chaps. "Uh... all what about?" she asked, feigning innocence.

Kristy grinned. "You don't fool me, RaeAnne." Her voice was low enough that only RaeAnne could hear her. "There's something going on between you and the hot cowboy. I practically saw sparks between you two."

RaeAnne adjusted her cap, then shielded her eyes from the sun, squinting so Kristy couldn't read her expression. The problem with being around friends was that they knew you too well. "I don't know what you're talking about."

"Fine. If that's the way you want to play it." Kristy set her tripod in position a tad bit harder than it needed to be.

Thankfully, she didn't pursue the subject. It wasn't one RaeAnne wanted to ponder. She moved closer to where Dan had set up his camera.

Dan was instructing Tyler where to move the horse so he wasn't in shadow, and then asked him to help Selena up.

Tyler boosted Selena into the saddle, then swung up easily behind her.

"Now, I need you both to look relaxed and happy." Dan adjusted the camera lens.

Selena smiled. Tyler smirked.

"No, no, Tyler," Dan protested. "A smile. A big smile."

Tyler smiled, but even RaeAnne could see it looked fake.

She really needed these photos—the whole article—to be perfect. She grit her teeth; Penny was a demanding editor.

5

"Try to look genuine," Dan coaxed. "I'll take a few experimental shots."

He did, but RaeAnne caught Dan's sigh, and his sigh said he wasn't happy with what he was seeing.

"Remember, we want people to see how beautiful the Palo Duro canyon can be," RaeAnne said in her most encouraging voice. "We want people to see a wonderful place to visit.! You should look like you're happy to be here."

"I'm always happy to be here." Tyler's smile looked sincere.

"That's it!" Dan snapped a couple of shots in quick succession. "Sean, take some from your angle. Kristy, you, too." He paused, and moved slightly. "Now, Selena, lean a little to your left. That's it. And Tyler, a little to your right." They moved, but Dan frowned. "Tyler, a little more to the left. And sit back slightly. Kristy, help him."

Kristy moved forward and attempted to position Tyler better.

"This isn't a natural. I wouldn't sit on my horse at this angle," he said.

"It's just for the photo. It may feel unnatural, but the photo will look natural in the end," RaeAnne reassured him.

His eyes met hers. Tingles shimmered down to her toes once again.

"Perfect!" Dan declared.

Kristy took a few rapid steps back and he moved the camera slightly and took three pictures in succession.

Then Selena flicked her hair back. "I'm thirsty," she announced.

"Damn. That was perfect," Dan groaned.

RaeAnne groaned along with him, but silently. She'd offered Selena some water less than five minutes ago and the woman had turned it down.

She went to the cooler by the folding chairs they'd set up near a beach umbrella. Reaching into the ice-filled cooler, she withdrew a bottle of water. She tried hard to keep her expression neutral as she handed it to Selena.

Selena took a long swig of water as Tyler looked on, frowning.

"Here." Selena thrust the bottle back at RaeAnne as if she were a queen and RaeAnne a peasant. She tossed her head "I'm ready."

Dan's expression of disgust was almost funny, but he quickly smoothed it out and went into professional mode once again.

He instructed Tyler and Selena to move slightly one way, then the other. Frowning, he took some more photos. "That's still not quite right."

"You want more photos?" Selena looked astonished. "Listen, you put me in this long-sleeved shirt here—"she pulled at one cuff—"and I'm damned uncomfortable in this heat."

"Because it looked like a typical western shirt," Kristy said, sounding defensive. "And stylish." The burnt orange, brown and blue plaid on a cream background looked perfect on Selena. "I do have a short-sleeved plaid here with us—"

"Never mind," Selena snapped.

"We do want you to blend in with this Texas setting," RaeAnne said. Selena was from Houston, and she had to be used to hot summers, so it couldn't be the long sleeves she was objecting to.

"Now hold still for some more photos," Dan said.

"Kristy, will you position Selena again? Tyler, stay as you are."

Kristy did, and Dan shifted slightly, trying to capture the best photo he could. He directed them to look up, then down, then up again. To the right, then the left. He snapped his camera, and Sean took photos from a different angle as Kristy stood by, positioning the two occasionally.

"Selena, bend forward just slightly. Your arm— move it an inch or so," Dan continued.

Tyler sighed. Loudly. RaeAnne felt sympathy well up in her. It couldn't be easy sitting still on a hot morning when he was used to riding his horse. The Golden Q, where they were photographing, was a working ranch but did offer trail rides on weekends to guests at his sister Missy's bed-and-breakfast. He was probably not used to spending a typical Tuesday sitting still.

"Kristy, can you reposition Selena?" Dan asked.

She moved forward, and Selena snapped, "I can move myself."

"You're not following what I said," Dan responded. "I need you to bend forward, then lift the reins a little—like this." He demonstrated.

"I am!" she shouted.

RaeAnne met Kristy's exasperated expression. She had heard that Selena wasn't the easiest model to work with but Penny had felt Selena's good looks would be perfect in their photos. She'd warned the team that they'd have to put up with some drama from Selena.

And when the Golden Q had sent the requested photos of the cowboys working there, Penny had selected Tyler at once as her first choice to pose with Selena.

"Now smile, Selena," Dan coaxed.

Her expression was decidedly not a smile—more like a grimace.

Dan's tone became even more placating. "C'mon, Selena, I know you can do this."

"Forget it!" This time she sounded super angry. Swinging down from the horse, she yelled, "I quit! I don't have to take this shit in this heat! I know how to model! I've quit better jobs than this!"

And Selena strode off, anger rolling off her in waves.

Oh shit! RaeAnne didn't need this.

Dan raised his eyebrows at her as numbness encased RaeAnne.

"What do we do now?" Kristy asked as Selena reached the umbrella and plopped onto a chair.

"Someone drive me back to the bed-and-breakfast," Selena commanded. "I'll pack up and head home."

Dan, Sean, Kristy and RaeAnne looked at each other. What were they going to do now? No, what was *she* going to do now? This article—this job—was her responsibility. RaeAnne's heart sunk lower and lower as she stared at the others.

This would horribly disappoint Penny. Or worse, Penny would be hopping mad. *And* they'd be behind schedule.

And she'd disappoint herself even more. Because this could be her opportunity to prove herself for Penny's job when Penny went on maternity leave.

She needed to talk Selena back into the saddle. She took a breath, pasted a smile on her face, then faced Selena.

"I'm not going to change my mind." Selena held up her hand before RaeAnne could even take a step.

9

Had this happened before? RaeAnne wondered. Was that why Selena's reputation was tarnished?

"I'm not going to take her back," Tyler said. "I have work to do on the ranch, and I'm taking the time to help you guys with these photos."

"I'll do it," Sean volunteered. He'd been staring at Selena since she arrived last night at Missy's bed and breakfast.

Dan had lost patience. "Yeah, Sean. Please get her out of my sight." As Sean loped off toward Selena, Dan swore. "Just my luck. We get a prima donna." Turning to RaeAnne, he blurted, "What do you want to do now?"

"Do?" Her words got stuck in her throat. What should she do? A cold, paralyzing fear crept through her. It was up to *her* to do something since Penny wasn't present. Perfect practice for the editor's job—but scary if she made the wrong decision.

"We'll have to… find another model," she stammered. "Or take the photos of Tyler alone—"

"No, we need to show that a tourist would have fun here with the ranchers and horses," Kristy interrupted. "You said that just yesterday when we arrived."

"Ugh—yes." Her thoughts in a whirl, she tried to think logically. Where could she get a model on short notice?

Dan was looking at her appraisingly. "You could be our model, RaeAnne."

She could model? *Her?* Get up on that horse with that handsome-as-sin, super hot cowboy?

And somehow hide the fact that she was attracted to him.

10

CHAPTER II

RaeAnne gasped out loud.

She knew she wasn't bad looking. Pretty and cute were how a few guys she'd dated had described her. But Selena was model-thin, truly gorgeous--and she wasn't anything like that.

"I—I can't—"

And just the thought of sitting together with that cowboy—another handsome, flirtatious cowboy like Ben—sent a shiver down her spine.

"Sure you can," Dan encouraged her.

"You can do it!" Kristy echoed. "You're not as tall as models like Selena but what's the big deal? You'll be on a horse. It's not like you're trying to be a fashion model."

"But I'm not—I'm not used to modeling—"

"How hard can it be?" Tyler's deep voice sent a curl of warmth up her spine.

She swallowed. "Isn't it a conflict of interest? I'm an assistant editor, not a model," she said, turning to Dan.

He shrugged. "Not as long as you agree and sign a model release form. After all, you want to get this done, right?"

"But I should ask Penny—"

11

"She'd say to get the job done as quickly as possible," Kristy declared.

It was true. Penny was a stickler for meeting deadlines.

"Besides, I don't have a lot of time to waste," Tyler added.

RaeAnne took a deep breath. Well. It looked like everyone was in agreement. And she did *not* want to let her editor down. Not with so much riding on this article—figuratively and literally.

Tyler fixed his brown eyes on her. "I'm sure you'll look great in the photos."

Well. She felt just a little flattered at his words.

"All right," she said, hearing the breathless note in her voice.

When Tyler smiled, her insides turned to mush.

She didn't need that.

He got off the horse. "I'll help you up."

"Wait. Take off your sunglasses," Kristy directed RaeAnne."

RaeAnne let her friend fuss around her, dabbing powder on her face, some lip gloss, and combing her blond hair.

"There." Kristy stepped away. "You look perfect."

RaeAnne grimaced slightly. Not quite, she thought. Pretty, yes, but beautiful... .?

Tyler grinned. "C'mon, I'll boost you up. You've ridden, right?"

"When I was a kid. I spent the first five years of my life near here," RaeAnne told him. "Now I ride at stables near my home."

"Oh, you're from the canyon?" He sounded impressed. "Where's home now?"

"Dallas. And yes."

She walked over and he gave her a boost up. She swung one foot over the horse.

She was struck by two things as he vaulted up behind her. The warmth radiating from him and his soapy, clean smell.

She wasn't happy about being so very aware of him. Every nerve in her body was energized, totally conscious of each detail about Tyler Quimby.

He leaned closer. She could feel his thighs behind her, strong and powerful.

Unbidden, images of Tyler hovering over her—in bed—invaded her mind.

Her mouth went dry.

She could feel his warmth. She felt his breath stir the air by her left ear. As she sucked in air, she smelled mint.

He was one appealing male!

She fought the thought, resisting his compelling presence.

"Comfortable?" he whispered, his voice a husky timbre.

"Uhm—yes." She didn't like the fact that she sounded like a schoolgirl.

Another good-looking cowboy, flirting with her. Normally she laughed it off and moved away.

But *I'm stuck in the saddle with you*, she thought.

Something tightened inside her at the thought, almost as if… as if she was *glad* to be stuck with him.

She pushed the thought aside mentally, and automatically took hold of the reins, her hands behind Tyler's.

Her hands trembled.

13

"That's it," Dan said. "Lean a little to the left, RaeAnne."

She did and felt Tyler's hand touch hers on the reins.

"Cover her hands with yours, Tyler," Dan directed.

As he did, she felt heat suffuse her. His hands were strong, yet they covered hers in a reassuring, not an intimidating, way.

"You can do this," he whispered, his tone encouraging.

"I'll try," she whispered back.

She could do this. She'd work with Dan and get the job done, fast. After all, the sooner Dan could take his photos, the sooner she could get out of this saddle.

She was tempted to lean into Tyler.

Dan was taking the shots, directing them for each one. "Smile wider," he encouraged. "Good. Good! RaeAnne, tilt your head a little."

She complied, wanting to be as professional as possible.

"Okay. Now, Tyler, I want you to smile at RaeAnne. RaeAnne, look up at him," Dan directed.

She obeyed. And felt a tremor move through her at Tyler's smile.

Without thinking, she smiled back.

"Perfect." Dan said, practically cheering. *Click. Click.* The camera snapped photos one after the other.

"Wow, that looks great," Kristy agreed.

It *felt* great. And suddenly, being in such close proximity to Tyler felt more wonderful than scary.

RaeAnne tightened her hands on the reigns, then realizing what she was doing, eased her grip so as to keep the horse calm.

But it was scary that she liked being so close to Tyler.

She swallowed. Since she was stuck with this handsome cowboy, she'd have to put up with these conflicting feelings. And hope the photo session ended soon.

"How about a couple with his cowboy hat?" Kristy asked.

"If it won't shadow his face too much," Dan replied.

Kristy grabbed the brown hat from a fence post then handed it to Tyler. He placed it on his head and both Kristy and Dan shot a few more photos from different angles.

After what seemed like a month, he said, "That's good, folks. Okay, you can get down. Tyler, I'd just like a few shots of you leading the horse, then we're done for this morning."

Relief flooded through RaeAnne.

Relief—and just a little disappointment. As Tyler moved, she felt the sudden coolness that replaced his firm body.

He slid off the horse and reached up to help her down.

She took his hands, and tingles danced up her arms . For a moment, she was tempted to stand there, in the circle of his arms.

This was not good. The last thing she wanted— especially in the middle of a job assignment—was an attraction to a handsome cowboy. A man who probably thought about horses and himself and ranching and little else.

Or… about women. Lots of women.

And even if he didn't—even if he was a truly nice

15

guy, which, based on his actions seemed possible—she didn't want any kind of involvement. Period.

With her family's track record— she swallowed at the thought, and RaeAnne stepped backward.

"I think Dan got some great shots," Kristy said.

"We'll know when he looks at everything later," RaeAnne said in a low tone so only Kristy could hear. "I sure hope so. I'd hate to have to do this all over again."

Kristy raised her eyebrows. "Really? I'd think you'd *want* to do it all over again. Sitting close to that hunk."

"I was stuck in the saddle with him," RaeAnne said rather brusquely. "It wasn't by choice."

Kristy just looked at her, eyebrows raised.

Sean was back from escorting Selena. "How's it going?"

Glad for the distraction, RaeAnne turned to him. "I think it went well. We'll know more after Dan examines the photos."

She hoped he had what he needed.

Dan finished taking the shots of Tyler leading the stallion, then Tyler swung onto his horse. "C'mon, Thunder. Bye, everyone," he added.

She had work to do herself. Glancing at her watch, she saw they still had some time before lunch.

"I'm going to walk around and see where else we can get some good shots," she told Dan. "Let's meet back here for lunch." Missy, the owner of the bed and breakfast where they'd stayed last night, had agreed to pack them lunches when they'd first contacted her.

"Okay," the others chorused.

"I'll scope out some possible locations, too," Dan said.

As she wandered around the barn and the

outbuildings, RaeAnne tried not to think about Tyler Quimby and instead concentrated on the colorful ranch before her and the spots which would make for good photos.

Men were leading horses into and out of the barn. A Hispanic woman was doing something by the chicken coop area. A couple of mixed breed dogs were laying in the shade, and a gray cat strolled out of the barn.

Some shots of the barn would be nice, she decided, and also a few pictures of life on a working ranch. Maybe even a few photos of the ranchers working, although that would not be a part of any tourist visit. Unless women like her just wanted to observe a good-looking cowboy.

As she strolled around, absorbing the sights, the smell of horses and leather, the sounds of neighing and cluck of chickens, the call of a bird she didn't recognize, the shimmering heat, she felt her body relaxing. The sensations were at once nostalgic and familiar. The overwhelming peace of the Palo Duro canyon began to sink into her body, into her bones. While it wasn't quiet, and the ranch was certainly busy with its normal activities, there was still an over-reaching sense of peace and quiet.

After the hustle and bustle of Dallas, a city she'd spent lots of time in, the peace here was a welcome change. People working with their hands, working with animals, with the land. She could smell and hear nature, not traffic. People actually called out to each other. Their noses weren't buried in their cell phones.

She paused by a fence and watched a slender cowboy walking his horse into the barn, speaking to the brown horse in a soothing voice.

17

"Here we go, Cocoa, time to rest for a while." He sent the horse a fond look, and the horse snuffled in answer.

Another cat, an orange one, left the barn. It blinked, gazed around, and apparently decided the shade of the barn was better than the mid-day heat. He turned and returned to the barn.

Enjoy this while you can, she told herself. Before she knew it she'd be back in her apartment in Dallas, commuting to her job with thousands of other people who lived and worked in the city.

Her stomach growled. She hadn't wanted too big a breakfast at the Bed & Breakfast—she was used to eating oatmeal with her coffee and then rushing around. So, she'd limited herself to one waffle and a peach with her coffee. But now she was getting hungry again. She'd worked up an appetite. A glance at her watch showed it was a few minutes after twelve already.

Turning, she headed back to the umbrella and cooler they'd brought with them.

Sean was already munching on a sandwich and Dan was reaching into the cooler for a bottle of water.

"As soon as we're done eating, I'm heading back to the B&B," he told her. "I'll spend the afternoon going over the photos and picking out the best ones. Then you can narrow them down further."

"Sounds good." RaeAnne slid into a chair in the shade. "Can you pass me a bottle of water?"

The cool bottle felt good against her warm palm. She drank quickly.

Kristy appeared behind her. "We have turkey, ham and cheese, or peanut butter and jelly sandwiches," she said.

"I'll take ham and cheese," RaeAnne told her friend.

As they ate, the four of them talked about the morning's shoot. Dan was angry at Selena's cavalier attitude. "It's so unprofessional," he complained.

"I'm going to tell Penny just what happened," RaeAnne said, "and recommend we never use her again. For anything."

"Yeah, what kind of professional walks off like that, right in the middle of a shoot?" Kristy said.

"Someone who's *not* a professional," RaeAnne answered.

They chatted about other models they'd worked with on *Texas Trails Magazine*.

"You were a good sport to step in for the photos." Dan changed the topic.

"Yeah, well... I didn't want to delay the schedule," she said.

"But I bet you wouldn't mind a few more minutes spent up there on the horse with Tyler," Kristy said.

"No, I didn't want to be stuck with him," RaeAnne protested.

"Why not?" her friend asked.

"Because I've had it with superficial, flirting cowboys," RaeAnne said firmly.

Which wasn't totally true... but close enough.

CHAPTER III

As he made his rounds supervising the other cowboys and checking the fence, Tyler couldn't keep his mind off RaeAnne Tilton, the curvy assistant editor who'd sat with him on his favorite horse, Thunder.

He'd been attracted to her from the moment he saw her—plain and simple—not that smooth, tall, high-falutin' model everyone had said was gorgeous.

Her face was not just pretty—it was quietly beautiful, and without loads of make-up like Selena wore. RaeAnne had thick, lustrous hair that was a silky blond--and green eyes fringed with dark lashes. Her lips were just begging to be kissed. She was short, and slim, but her simple blue T-shirt revealed a generous bust that any man would want to bury his face in.

He'd liked her positive attitude in the face of a major problem. And when Dan had suggested she sit in front of him—he'd actually been delighted.

She'd seemed pretty hesitant to get on the horse with him. Since she'd said she'd ridden before, it didn't seem to be any fear of horses. She must have been hesitant to sit by *him*. Was she shy? Just afraid to model for the magazine? Or something else?

Having her in front of him had been more than

tempting. He liked the feel of her hands under his and could imagine having more of her under him.

In fact, his imagination could run wild if he let it. He'd had to force himself to reign in all thoughts like that and concentrate on the boring job of looking good for the photos.

The photos were a timesuck , but he'd been asked to do it. He wasn't thrilled with the thought of an article bringing more visitors to the Palo Duro canyon, one of the most peaceful places on God's green earth. But it would bring visitors to his sister Missy's bed-and-breakfast, the Bluebonnet Inn, and that was important to her—so, consequently, to him.

Missy had been widowed a little over two years ago, just a year after she and her husband Lew had bought the B&B. Lew had been young—only 32—two years older than Missy. His death had been tragic, only months after being diagnosed with cancer. Their daughters had been two and four at the time, so Missy desperately needed the B&B to do well so she could support her family.

Of course, their parents and his brother Clay and he all wanted to pitch in, but Missy, the oldest of the three siblings, wanted to do this on her own. He had to respect that.

So he was willing to spend a couple of hours on photos if it would help Missy.

But once the stuck-up model had left, it hadn't seemed like a waste of time. He had enjoyed being on horseback with RaeAnne, even if the pose of her in the saddle, with him behind, was a little awkward.

Because he'd enjoyed every moment of sitting with her.

And if he could get to see RaeAnne again, it'd definitely be worth it—

So it was pretty convenient that the magazine crew was staying at Missy's.

He remembered Missy saying something about cooking one night for the crew. A quick call to his sister confirmed that tonight was the night.

In fact, Clay, who liked competing on the barbeque circuit, had barbecued chicken and Missy had made home made potato salad and coleslaw to go with the meal.

It wasn't hard to wrangle an invitation to dinner from her.

At the end of the afternoon, he and his crew wrapped up work. He drove to his home on the far reaches of the Golden Q property—the ranch home he'd had built just three years ago—and took a quick shower, changing into clean jeans and another T-shirt before heading to Missy's in his truck.

Missy's B&B was in the next town, Claude, only about a 15 minute ride. When he arrived, she was setting the table

"Hey, squirts," Tyler said to his nieces, Angie and Patty.

"Hi, Uncle Tyler!" they replied. Angie was putting a napkin by each chair in the dining room while Missy brought over a platter laden with their brother, Clay's, award-winning barbecued chicken. Patty watched her older sister.

Tyler's mouth watered at the sight and smell of the spicy chicken. His brother's signature glaze included his weird combo of grape jelly, ketchup, and spices.

"Perfect timing," Missy said as he gave her a quick kiss. "So you didn't feel like cooking tonight?"

"Nah, and I didn't want to eat at Mom and Dad's," he said. "Clay would be busting my chops about being a model." Clay was twenty-seven, three years younger than him, and a big tease. "And Mom and Dad would have loads of questions."

"I have a few, too," Missy teased. "I told the crew to come down at six and—"she glanced at her watch— "it's three minutes of. Could you grab the pitchers from the fridge?"

He brought over the sweet tea, lemonade, and ice water, and put them on the table. He heard footsteps coming downstairs, and looked up to see Dan, followed by the rest of the photo crew. Including RaeAnne.

And she looked just as pretty as she had this morning.

Tyler maneuvered himself so he was sitting to RaeAnne's left, with Angie on her right. His sister sat at the head of the table with her kids on either side of her. On the opposite side of the table were Sean and Kristy, and Dan was at the bottom on his left.

Missy started the conversation rolling by asking about the photo shoot.

Dan passed the platter of chicken as he described the difficulties of working with the top model, Selena, and replacing her with RaeAnne.

"RaeAnne was a champ, though." Dan helped himself to a large spoonful of potato salad. "I've spent the afternoon going over the shots and I've got some good ones. I'll show you later," he told RaeAnne.

Disappointment slid through Tyler. He'd hoped to take a few more photos with RaeAnne.

Dan added, "I'd like to take a few more shots tomorrow by the barn." He looked at Tyler. "You have some time?"

"Sure," Tyler tried to hide the fact that his nerve endings leapt with excitement at Dan's words.

"Okay," RaeAnne agreed, helping herself to his sister's delicious coleslaw.

Tyler selected a piece of chicken. "Wait 'til you taste this," he bragged. The spicy and sweet aroma reached out to him, and everyone else at the table. "Our brother Clay made it."

"He competes in barbeque contests," Missy added.

"How many siblings do you have?" RaeAnne asked, turning to look at Tyler.

"Missy, Clay and I," he said. "Missy's the oldest, than me, than Clay. Clay and I work on our dad's ranch."

"You'll probably see our parents at some point over there," Missy spooned potato salad on her daughters' plates.

The food smelled delicious, and once his plate was full, Tyler dug in. He was hungrier than usual. He got the feeling his senses were on alert, because everything tasted even better than usual.

"Mmm, this is good," RaeAnne said, after taking a taste of the chicken.

Tyler caught a whiff of the perfume she'd been wearing this morning. It smelled a little like coconut, subtle and it suited her.

Her thick hair shone in the dining room lights and he flexed his fingers. He had the strongest desire to run his fingers through that gorgeous, blonde hair.

RaeAnne's hair had a natural glow. Not a straight-out-of-the-bottle, fake blonde like that model's almost white hair.

"What's it like in the Palo Duro canyon area?" Sean asked.

"Nice," Missy answered.

"It's pretty quiet here," Tyler told him. "And life isn't always easy. Hot, dry summers. Cold, windy winters. But we love the peace here in the canyon."

Missy turned to RaeAnne. "Someone said you lived in these parts when you were little." She passed a roll to Patty.

RaeAnne hesitated, then said, "Yes. Until I was five and my father was—was killed in a car accident. He was hit by a drunk driver." She shivered.

Tyler's heart went out to her. He couldn't imagine how he'd feel if he lost his dad. Like his nieces... He tried not to look at Missy; it was still tough for her.

"I lived about twenty minutes from here," RaeAnne continued. "But when my father died, my mother packed up me and my sister and moved us to Houston where she was from. She still had family there."

"So you must be one of the Tiltons from over in Long Valley?" Missy asked. "I went to school with an Emma Tilton."

RaeAnne nodded. "One of my cousins on my father's side. I believe her father was first cousin to mine. Ed Tilton. And she has three brothers and a sister."

"Yes, that's the one. It's good to have you back," Missy said.

So RaeAnne really was a canyon girl. "Do you remember much about living here?" Tyler questioned.

RaeAnne sipped her sweet tea. "Now that I'm here, things are coming back to me. The red dust, for instance. And all the wildflowers we don't see in Dallas, which is where I live now."

"Any of you others grow up around here?" Missy asked, glancing around the table.

"No. San Antoine," Sean said.

"Dallas," Kristy answered.

"The Cleveland area," Dan told them.

"You've come a long way," Missy said.

He grinned. "I went to University of Houston, liked Texas, and decided to stay here. I got the job with *Texas Trails* in Dallas after working for a small newspaper near Dallas."

"I went to Texas Tech," Missy said, "and so did Clay. Tyler went to Texas A&M University. What about the rest of you?" Her gaze swung around the table.

"University of New Mexico," RaeAnne said. "They have a great journalism program. In fact, best-selling teen author, Lois Duncan, taught some classes there."

That statement veered the conversation to talk about books they'd read and how the movies weren't as good. Missy's girls joined in with a few comments about Disney movies. As they spoke, Tyler studied RaeAnne. She talked in a positive, animated manner, yet she appeared to be a calm person.

Once, when he asked her to pass the bowl of coleslaw, her fingers touched his.

And zap! He was zinged by the same electricity he'd felt earlier in the day. Maybe it was even stronger now.

He watched RaeAnne, but all she displayed was a neutral expression.

He *wanted* her to feel it too. He determined he would spend time alone with her after dinner.

Missy announced they had blueberry pie, baked by their mom, for dessert plus ice cream.

Afterward, they all helped Missy clear the table.

"Guests shouldn't have to help," Missy protested.

"With all of us here, it will be faster if we do," RaeAnne said. "Besides, you normally don't make dinners for your guests—you're doing us a big favor. Tomorrow, I think we're all going into town to eat at the diner for supper so you won't have any extra work." She smiled at Missy.

And just like that, Tyler's heart slid deeper into a pool of… something. More than simple attraction.. Strong liking? He liked the fact that she was considerate of his sister. He'd met too many superficial women.

"Why don't you all go enjoy the pool?" Missy invited as she collected plates. "On a hot summer night like this, it's beautiful."

"I want to do a little more work," Dan said, bringing two empty bowls into the kitchen.

"I think I will," RaeAnne said.

"Me, too," Sean said.

Tyler was glad he'd brought his bathing suit. "I'm going to. I haven't put a pool my house yet, and when I'm at Mom and Dad's, Dad just wants to talk business all the time." And his Mom was always questioning him about when he was going to find a nice girl and settle down. But then, she was a confirmed romantic. As was his dad.

27

He changed in the downstairs bathroom. When he walked into the backyard, the sun had dipped low and insects were buzzing. Missy had lit a citronella candle to keep the worst of the bugs away, and the scent made his nose twitch. Sean had already changed and was swimming in the pool.

"Where are RaeAnne and Kristy?" he asked, slipping into the delightfully cool water.

Sean treaded water. "They said they'd be down in a few."

It was at least fifteen minutes before the women arrived.

But it was worth the wait.

While Kristy was on the skinny side and a lot of men would like her looks in a black bikini, which contrasted with her light brown hair, RaeAnne looked all woman.

The light blue bikini she wore showed off generous, but not overly large, breasts, a small waist, and thighs that were just the right size.

He swallowed, his throat suddenly dry.

He dove into the water, hoping to cool his thoughts as well as his body.

When he surfaced, RaeAnne was dropping her towel on a chaise. She walked over and sat on the edge of the pool, sliding her feet into the water up to her knees. RaeAnne must have sensed his intent look, because she met Tyler's eyes. He smiled, hoping he didn't look like some eager kid impressed by a gorgeous body.

Her body was gorgeous. And he was impressed. He just didn't want to seem like a gawky teenager.

Although he felt like one.

CHAPTER IV

RaeAnne couldn't help staring at Tyler in his navy swimming trunks.

He was long and lean, yet his shoulders were muscular. The setting sun brought out highlights that were almost red in his dark, wavy hair.

Why did she have to work with such an appealing cowboy?

And it wasn't just his looks. The man was *nice*. She could see the affectionate, caring way he spoke to his sister and nieces and the friendly way he spoke to her and the rest of the crew.

Kristy had left the pool and stretched out on a chaise with her ear buds in, probably listening to her favorite, Tim McGraw. Sean was doing slow laps. Tyler was treading water in front of her, but, as she dangled her feet in the cool water, letting it take away some of the heat of the day, he swam up to her.

"C'mon in," he invited.

"I will," she said. "When I adjust to the cool water."

The outside air was still hot, though, just a more tolerable heat than the daytime temperature.

She and Kristy had driven around for two hours this

afternoon, looking for other places to take photos of the scenery, trying to recognize places where her favorite TV show—"The Cattle Drive"—had been filmed.

And Kristy had wondered about Tyler.

"He's so cute," she'd said. "And he must be about your age, RaeAnne."

RaeAnne had shot her a look. "You know I don't want to get involved again."

"You won't feel that way forever," Kristy predicted. "I'll tell you, if I didn't have Billy"—who was her current beau—"I'd be making a play for him. Do you know if he's single?"

RaeAnne had shook her head. "He may be, but I don't know for sure."

Now, though, she wondered. "You said you were planning to put in a pool," she said, knowing she was being nosy. "You built your own house? Do you live there with your brother—or someone else?"

Not that it should matter, a little voice inside her said.

"I live alone," he said. "Right now, my brother is planning to build his own house in another year. And I don't have a girlfriend, if you're wondering."

She felt herself flushing.

"Not that I would mind one if the right girl came along," he drawled.

Was that smile just for her?

Of course, he probably smiled like that at every woman he flirted with.

Too bad that smile was so appealing.

She slid into the pool, hoping to cool herself down.

"I'm sure you'll find someone," she said in the

most neutral tone she could force out. The water lapped at her body.

"Do you think that will be difficult?" he asked, quirking his eyebrows, his tone humorous.

"Not at all," she said without thinking. Then, hearing her own words, she chastised herself silently. "Ugh, that is—I'm sure a handsome cowboy like you won't have any trouble finding a girlfriend."

"You think I'm handsome?" He grinned at her, swimming closer.

She glanced away. "You obviously are. I'm sure girls are chasing you all the time. You don't have to ask me that question."

"Yes, I do." His tone had grown more serious.

She looked back at him. Darkness was falling rapidly, and in the shadows, she saw the searching look on his face.

He drew closer, and since they were standing in only about four feet of water, he stood up. But she'd swear she could feel his heat through the cool water and warm air. He positively radiated warmth.

"Do *you* think I'm handsome, RaeAnne?"

"I—" she paused. "Yes. You're handsome." Very much so.

He smiled. "And I think—" He cupped her chin. "And I think you're beautiful, RaeAnne."

Now her whole body was flushing, not just her face. Where he touched her, she felt warmth, which sank into her chin, into her very bones. Warmth and something else—something intangible. Caring? But how could that be? They barely knew each other.

"I bet you say that to all the girls." She tried to sound light-hearted.

31

"No." He shook his head. "Only the ones who are beautiful, and *only* the ones who are nice people, too."

She raised her eyebrows. "How do you know I'm a nice person?"

He laughed, and let go of her chin. "I can tell. The way you talk to your co-workers, the way you are friendly to my sister and nieces. Hell, you were even nice and calm to that conceited model, Selena."

"Oh." She wasn't sure what else to say. Sure, she tried to be nice. She prided herself on being a good person, the kind someone would want for a friend. Was he just giving her a line, empty flattery? Was he another smooth-talkin' cowboy like Ben? "Uhm... thanks," she muttered.

"I mean it."

She headed to the deep end of the pool, refusing to succumb to silly flattery and flirting just because he was handsome as sin. He followed her.

A phone rang and Kristy grabbed it. "Hi Billy!" She slid into her flip flops and headed inside.

RaeAnne asked, "tell me about your sister, and your family. How long ago was she widowed? She's young."

"She's thirty-two, two years older than me. She was widowed a couple of years ago, and yeah, she was young." Bitterness crept into his voice. "It was cancer—and he went very suddenly."

"I'm so sorry." She meant it. "I lost an aunt to cancer last year. It sucks."

"Yeah." He looked down for a moment, then met her eyes. "My brother is twenty-seven. We're all pretty close. We grew up here in the canyon, and we love it. It's home with a capital H."

She swam to the side of the pool, and climbed the half ladder. She felt refreshed by the short swim, and the air seemed cooler now. Or maybe it was just that she was more comfortable after her dip in the pool. "Tell me about your parents. Did they always live around here?" She perched at the side of the pool.

Sean got out of the pool at the same moment, reached for a towel, and called goodnight as he went inside.

"My dad did," Tyler said. "He, his father, and his grandfather. My great-great grandfather came from Pennsylvania and moved out here sometime in the 1860s, we think. But my mother is from New Jersey."

"New Jersey? How'd she end up here?" RaeAnne asked.

He swam to the edge, and hefted himself out of the water, sitting beside her. He slung a towel over his shoulders. Even after his swim, she caught the scent of fresh, woodsy aftershave.

His close proximity, his fresh, masculine scent, and the darkness surrounding them were a strong combination. The tiki light flared suddenly, and the faintest trace of smoke floated towards them. It was a lovely setting, the air charged with something, the atmosphere as romantic as all get-out.

And she wanted to get out. Literally. She didn't want to feel him close, to feel this attraction, this sense of something—romantic.

His laugh, deep and pleasant, interrupted her thoughts. "Long story. My mom's fourth grade teacher did a pen pal project with a friend of hers who taught near here. She began corresponding with my aunt, Betty Lou. They became fast friends, and continued

33

writing to each other even when they were teens, even when my mom started commuting to college and my aunt got a job as a secretary. When my aunt was getting married, she felt so close to my mom—Abby—that she invited her to be one of her bridesmaids.

"My mom made her own gown, from a pattern my aunt chose. And she came down for the wedding, and that's the first time they actually met in person, and they still hit if off like sisters. Then she met my aunt's older brother, my dad, Jim."

He smiled, and RaeAnne found herself smiling too. "And they fell for each other?"

"My father said he took one look at her and knew she was *the one*. My mother said she knew when they danced together at Betty Lou and Tommy's wedding."

"How romantic." She felt a weird sensation. Could it be envy? How wonderful and simple love could be. For *some* people.

Unfortunately, not for her. She sighed.

He cocked an eyebrow. "Do you believe in love at first sight?

"Love at first sight?" she echoed, looking into his face, which was brimming with positive energy. *Yes. No.* "I don't think so."

Something flickered across his face. Disappointment? "It was true for my parents," he stated.

"They're the exception, then."

"I've heard of other cases, too. There's my friend, Keith. He met someone at a party, and they've been together ever since. And—"

"So your mother stayed in Texas?" She needed to get off this topic.

"Well, they had their challenges. She went back to

Bayonne, NJ, and of course her family wasn't thrilled when she announced she was moving to Texas and leaving college. She didn't listen, though. She moved here—my grandparents said she could live in Betty Lou's old room—and enrolled in a local college. They got married a year later, and she finished college part-time, then taught for a couple of years until they had Missy."

"That's a nice story," RaeAnne said lightly. It was. A twinge of envy moved up her spine. If only her own life could be so simple and positive!

"It's true."

She met his eyes, and something in his expression took her breath away.

He leaned closer. His mouth hovered near hers. "I believe in love at first sight," he whispered. She could feel his warm breath skim across her face. "It happened to my parents. I think it could happen to me."

His lips brushed hers.

A jolt of pure electricity shot through her.

His lips were warm, and as they brushed hers again, she felt an almost magnetic pull toward him. The warm air cushioned them, and she smelled flowers, blocking the smell from the citronella candle.

She also smelled pure male, woodsy and clean.

"Goodnight, Uncle Tyler!" a childish voice announced behind them.

And just like that, she snapped back to reality.

They both parted, and found the two little girls in their pajamas.

"They wanted to say goodnight," Missy said, apologetic.

Did she realize they had interrupted a kiss? RaeAnne forced herself not to squirm.

Tyler stood up. "Goodnight, squirts." He hugged each one.

"I'm going to bed, too," Missy told them. "Goodnight, Tyler. RaeAnne." She took the girls by the hand and led them back into the house.

"Goodnight," RaeAnne called after them.

Saved by the bell. RaeAnne took a deep breath.

She'd almost kissed Tyler.

Heck, she *had* kissed Tyler. It had been a mere touching of the lips, but it had been a kiss all the same. And it held the promise of more to come.

If they hadn't been interrupted, Tyler would have deepened the kiss.

She scrambled up "I think I'll turn in, too," she said hastily. She had to get away from Tyler. Had to get away from the temptation of this good looking cowboy.

A cowboy who also appeared to be a nice guy.

Grabbing her towel and cell phone, she said, "Goodnight," and hurried into the house.

She would shower, get into her pjs, and call Tara, her best friend. They'd met their freshman year at college and she could talk to her about anything.

Including hot cowboys.

But when she got out of the bathroom and passed Kristy's room, her friend waved to her. "C'mon in. Tell me what you thought of Tyler," she said.

RaeAnne perched on the bed and regarded Kristy.

Kristy was two years younger than RaeAnne, but they had gotten friendly over a year ago when they met in a dance/exercise class they were taking. Kristy, despite her youth, was a recovering alcoholic. She'd come from a family of top achievers—all lawyers, accountants, CEOs and doctors—who felt her choice of photography as a career wasn't good enough. She'd turned to liquor, unfortunately, to console herself for the constant put-downs and belittling of her choices— and not just in careers either. She was a non-conformist in a family of conformists, and she'd confided in RaeAnne that she didn't fit in and hated that she was not given respect or emotional support.

But she was working valiantly to make a better life for herself, a healthier one, and RaeAnne admired that. So when an assistant photographer's opening came up at "Texas Trails" magazine, she'd brought in some samples of Kristy's work and shown them to Dan and the art department. Kristy had landed the job.

RaeAnne had never regretted her staunch support for her friend. She believed in Kristy's recovery completely

And Kristy had been grateful that RaeAnne trusted her, a former alcoholic, to do good work for the magazine.

They sat now and discussed the day, and RaeAnne was glad to talk to someone, since Tara was far away in New Mexico.

"What do you think of Tyler?" Kristy asked, her expression curious.

"He's very nice," RaeAnne admitted. "And really handsome." She stopped there. She was reluctant to admit, even to her friend, that she was super attracted to Tyler.

"That's putting it mildly," Kristy agreed. "And I get the feeling he's very attracted to you, RaeAnne."

Pleasure flowed through her at her friend's words.

She had to admit she liked the thought that Tyler was attracted to her.

Even though she shouldn't, she told herself.

Ben's handsome face flashed in her mind.

"What is it?" her friend asked.

She made a face. "Just thinking about—Ben. I don't want to—get mixed up with another handsome cowboy."

"I know," Kristy said, and sighed. "I know how you feel. But not everyone is like Ben."

RaeAnne stared into the distance.

As far as she knew, Tyler could be *exactly* like Ben.

* * *

RaeAnne's alarm went off early the next morning, but at least she'd slept well in the comfortable bed at the B&B. She sat up, recalling the events of yesterday in a flash.

She'd ended the day with a shower, followed by a long call to Tara, and they'd stayed on almost an hour. Tara's advice had been simple: "Why don't you enjoy your time with Tyler? Have a fling? You don't want to get too involved, so don't. Just enjoy it for the moment."

RaeAnne hadn't been convinced about this advice, but she'd promised Tara she'd at least consider it.

They had another photo shoot this morning. It was her responsibility to make sure things went smoothly.

RaeAnne got dressed, selecting a short-sleeved purple top and denim capris. She opened her door, and stepped into the hall, just as Kristy was coming out of her room. They greeted each other, and proceeded downstairs to the dining room.

Missy had a nice breakfast laid out already. Toast, muffins, scrambled eggs, sausage. There were also small boxes of popular cereals set out, along with milk. Sean was already seated at the table, eating.

RaeAnne went over to the coffee immediately and poured herself a mug, adding milk and sugar. Kristy helped herself to a tea bag and made tea.

"I slept great," Sean said as they seated themselves at the table. "It's nice and quiet here."

"Yes, and peaceful," Kristy added.

RaeAnne nodded. "This is a nice place to stay."

Dan entered the room, and they began chatting about today's planned photos.

In the afternoon, when it was too hot to do much picture-taking, Kristy and RaeAnne were going to drive around again and look for some more locations that may have been used in filming "The Cattle Drive."

After breakfast, they packed up Dan's equipment and headed out in Dan's truck and RaeAnne's car to the site they'd been at yesterday. Dan set up, and took a few photos, pausing to move his cameras and try different angles. He muttered to himself as he tried one angle, then another. Sean and Kristy stood close by, making notes or helping him make adjustments.

RaeAnne's attention wandered as they worked. She couldn't help thinking about Tyler. His broad shoulders. His handsome face. His deep voice, and his laugh.

Their almost-kiss.

She shivered in the hot sun, remembering the sparks that had flowed through her at his gentle touch.

"Hello."

The voice behind her startled her so she almost dropped her clipboard. Whirling, she found Tyler.

"Hello," she said, her voice sounding almost breathless.

He smiled at her and something inside her fluttered.

"Can you bring the horse over here?" asked Dan, who was standing near a tree. Wildflowers grew around the tree's base, and a yellow butterfly flapped its wings as it settled on one of the purple flowers.

"Sure thing." Tyler winked at her, then led his black horse to where Dan indicated.

RaeAnne's phone buzzed and she dug it from her pocket.

Penny.

"Just a minute. It's Penny," she called to Dan.

"Hi Penny," she greeted her boss, as wind suddenly whistled through the air.

She'd called Penny yesterday afternoon to tell her about the debacle with Selena Lawrence. But Penny was in her usual Tuesday meeting with the art and graphics departments of the magazine. And Stella, the receptionist, had informed RaeAnne that Penny had to leave right after that to go to a wake for her uncle who had died.

"How are things going?" Penny asked in her usual hyper voice.

"Fine," RaeAnne said, hoping to keep Penny calm. "Except for one problem, which Dan solved."

"Oh? What was it?"

"Selena Lawrence didn't like the heat or the job and she walked off. She quit."

"Shit. What a jerk." Penny huffed. "She was perfect for the photos, and we were paying her good money."

"I know," RaeAnne said, hoping to soothe Penny.

"I'd heard she could be difficult, but I figured, this wasn't too hard a job—and really, we were paying her well—" Penny was practically yelling.

"Yes," RaeAnne agreed. She observed Kristy watching her, and grimaced at her friend.

Penny ranted for another two minutes, and then asked, "so what did you do? You said Dan solved the problem?"

"He asked me to step in."

"What?" Penny squawked.

RaeAnne repeated patiently, "I posed on horseback for some of the photos."

There was a moment of silence. "How did the photos look?" Penny asked.

"Actually, Dan was quite pleased," RaeAnne said, her heart beating hard. She liked this job, and wanted to keep it. "He went over the photos afterwards and again last night. He's only taking a few more landscapes out here today and a couple more with the cowboy, Tyler."

"Well, okay." Penny sounded mollified. "As long as we get good photos, I don't have any objection to your stepping in." There was another pause. "Thank you, RaeAnne."

"You're welcome." Relief ran through her. Penny was happy, and if she was happy, they could all be happy.

Penny was a rather demanding boss. Not unfair—just exacting.

RaeAnne smiled into the phone. "Except for the incident with Selena, things are going well."

"Good. Okay, I gotta run," Penny said abruptly. "I'll reach out to you tomorrow or Friday."

41

"Talk to you then," RaeAnne said, and the phone went silent as Penny hung up.

Pocketing her cell phone, RaeAnne took another deep breath, just as the red dust began to swirl from a gust of wind. She coughed and reached for her water bottle.

Tyler was just getting off his horse a few yards away. "You okay, RaeAnne?" he asked.

"Yes." She drank some water.

"You really did forget about the dust hereabouts?" he asked with a smile.

"Um... yes, I did."

Dan was adjusting something on one camera. "Okay, I'd like a few more shots of the two of you," he declared. "Now Sean, you take some landscape photos."

As RaeAnne watched, the three split up in different directions, each carrying a camera. Kristy headed to the barn, Sean to the bunk house, and Dan directed her and Tyler to a nearby fence.

"I know my sister packed you all a lunch," Tyler said. "What are y'all doing for supper?"

"We planned to go into town. Your sister said there's a great diner there," RaeAnne said.

"How 'bout if my brother and I join you?" Tyler asked.

She hesitated.

On one hand, the thought of having dinner with him again was exciting. On the other, she didn't want to get too excited.

But if the four of them were there with him—and his brother—it wasn't exactly a date. It was merely a group thing.

"O… okay," she agreed.

"Do you know how to get there?"

"Missy drew us a map this morning," she told him."Since she said GPS and cellphones don't work too well hereabouts."

"Great." He grinned. "What time are y'all gettin' there?"

"Around six-fifteen," she answered.

"I'll see you then." He smiled, then added, "Let's get you on Thunder."

Dan posed them and snapped a dozen photos, moving them slightly after each one. RaeAnne felt totally aware of Tyler behind her—his firm body, hearing and feeling his breath on her cheek. She caught the same woodsy aftershave he'd worn yesterday.

She could almost feel his lips on hers again, and swallowed hard.

"That's good, very good," Dan said. "Okay, that's a wrap, guys."

Tyler swung off Thunder, then helped her down.

She had notes to make on her article, and she knew he had work to get to. She smiled at him.

He smiled too. "See you later."

He led Thunder away, with that totally sexy swagger…

The swagger she was *not* going to notice.

CHAPTER IV

After jotting down notes for her article during the morning, RaeAnne spent the afternoon with Kristy scouting out locations to photograph on the weekend, while Dan and Sean went over the photos from today and yesterday.

RaeAnne found herself growing excited. Her book project, *Filming The Cattle Drive*, already had interest from one publisher of cinematography history. She'd done quite a bit of research on the old TV show, a very popular one in the early nineteen-sixties. She was familiar with the show and enthusiastic about their story lines and the actors. Her research had shown that at least four episodes had been shot around the Palo Duro canyon, with at least two others in nearby towns. Capturing some of those settings now for her book would be a plus.

Kristy had agreed to do the photography to go along with her narratives. And as long as they did most of the work on the weekend, Penny had no objection.

They had time off now in the afternoons since it was just too hot for Dan and the others to take photos, so she was using the time in her air conditioned jeep to merely drive to a few locations and see if they met her needs.

It was a productive afternoon. They located one

setting which she was certain was used in episode sixty-six, and another she was fifty percent sure of from episode forty-two. She just had to go back and look at her DVDs.

Returning to the B&B, she found Dan and Sean done working, relaxing with video games. Dan reported that they had some great photos to be used in this aspect of the article. "Tomorrow we can go over to Claude for some town shots," he told her. "And the following day I'm going to take some photos of the B&B and surrounding area."

She and Kristy showered off the red dust and heat of the day. RaeAnne changed to another pair of jeans, a short sleeved yellow top, and added her favorite hoop earrings and a couple of bracelets. She had enough time to sit down and do an outline of the info for the article.

They took one car, with Sean driving. Arriving at Trixie's Diner, they entered the brightly lit place which was humming with voices and brimming with delectable smells.

Tyler was waiting for them inside, along with a man who looked a lot like him, but younger, and whose eyes were hazel, not deep brown.

"This is my brother, Clay." He introduced the young man, and there were greetings and handshakes all around.

Tyler suggested they pick a booth towards the back where there were several large ones.

Kristy led the way with RaeAnne right behind her and Tyler following close behind. As they walked, she noticed a couple in one of the front booths. They were holding hands across the table, and RaeAnne couldn't help observing the look of love passing between them.

Tyler said, "This is our deputy, Josh Able, and his fiancée, Sunny."

The couple turned and said hello to all of them. Their smiles were as sunny as Sunny's name.

RaeAnne felt a tug in her gut—a feeling of envy. Would a man ever look at her the way Josh had gazed at Sunny?

Would she ever be able to gaze back as lovingly without the shadows of the past crowding in on her?

* * *

Tyler wondered at the expression that had flitted across RaeAnne's face.

Even watching her face in profile, he had seen that strange look. An expression of—envy, maybe—as he introduced his friends.

He hadn't seen that look on anyone else's face as he glanced around. Only on RaeAnne's.

Tyler slid in next to her now, his thigh just touching hers. It felt comfortable. Better than comfortable. As if they *should* be this close and touching each other.

"What do you recommend?" Dan asked as the waitress passed out menus.

"All y'all are new here, right?" she asked. "Are you those folks from the magazine takin' pictures of the canyon?"

"Yes," RaeAnne and Dan said simultaneously. "We're doing a feature on some small towns in the panhandle," RaeAnne added.

The waitress beamed at them.

"I recommend the cheeseburger platter," Tyler told Dan.

After studying the menu, they ordered. Tyler was pleased to learn that RaeAnne was also going to try his favorite—the cheeseburger deluxe platter.

She ordered a diet cola, though, while he opted for a chocolate milkshake.

He found himself studying her. What was that expression that had crossed her face? Who was this beautiful woman, really? What made her tick?

After collecting their menus, the waitress departed, promising to deliver their drinks swiftly.

Sean and Clay struck up a conversation about the Dallas Rangers' chances for this baseball season.

Clay sent Tyler a look before answering. He'd been teasing Tyler all day, ever since Eddie, one of their employees, had mentioned to Clay that Tyler looked like he was "taken by that pretty little blonde girl" when they'd been working together yesterday.

Clay's teasing hadn't fazed him, though. He teased Clay plenty when he had the opportunity.

And it wasn't going to stop him from trying to get to know RaeAnne better.

Glad for the opportunity to speak one-on-one with her, Tyler turned to regard her. "So you've heard about my family," he said quietly. "Tell me about yours."

She made a face. "Do you really want to know?"

"Yes," he answered. "I do."

"I'll tell you later," she said hastily, and glanced around the table.

He got the feeling that she didn't want to talk in front of a lot of people. Although, her co-workers probably knew something about her, wouldn't they?

"Here we are." Their waitress, Lou, had returned, balancing a tray. She handed out dinners—cheeseburgers

47

for him, RaeAnne, Clay and Dan; the meatloaf special for Sean; and a turkey club sandwich for Kristy.

He dug into his meal with gusto. But all the while, he watched RaeAnne.

She was still maintaining some distance from him. Which was hard, in the crowded booth. It was as if she was reluctant to let her thigh touch his.

Maybe she was shy around guys.

Whatever it was, he wasn't about to be discouraged. He liked RaeAnne. Hell, he was very attracted to her, too.

And he wanted to get to know her better.

She bit into the cheeseburger. "This is good," she said, sounding impressed.

"Excellent," Dan agreed.

Talk turned to the canyon and photo opportunities there. Dan and Sean detailed some of the landscape shots they'd taken.

"It is beautiful here in a stark way," Sean said.

"And it is all year round too," Clay added.

"What's it like during the winter?" RaeAnne questioned. "I was only five when we moved, and it was usually spring or summer when I visited my grandparents, so I honestly don't remember."

"Cold," Tyler answered. "And lots of snow."

"We get snow in Dallas," RaeAnne told him.

"Yeah, but there's more here. It can get real deep. And the wind—it goes right through you."

"Yeah, it's great for cuddling up by the fireplace in winter." Clay winked at her.

She flushed.

Tyler kicked his brother. Clay grinned.

Just wait 'til you like some girl, Tyler thought.

"I do remember making snowmen when we were little," RaeAnne said. "And, of course, watching 'The Cattle Drive' with my dad, after we'd come in and gotten warmed up. He loved those reruns. It was his favorite show."

"You know they filmed some episodes around here," Tyler said. "Like the one where Kirk Dawson played a bank robber who was trying to hide out on the drive."

"Yes, it was called *The Disguised Drover*," RaeAnne said.

"You must know that show well," Tyler said, his estimation of her going up even more.

"Well, I watched it so much—even after my dad died, I'd watch it and think of him," she admitted. "In fact, I'm working on a book about the show, with photos of the locations where it was filmed."

He leaned towards her. "Really? That's fascinating."

Clay made a snorting sound that only he could hear.

Tyler ignored him. "Tell me—"

"Hello!" An annoying female voice interrupted them.

Just the person he had no desire to see.

Doreen Hampson.

She'd been flirting with him for years but he tried to avoid her whenever possible. Unfortunately, she'd been trying a lot harder lately to get her claws into him.

"Hi, Dorrie," Clay said.

"Well, y'all must be new around here," she drawled, smiling at Sean.

Good. Let her concentrate on the newcomers.

"These are some people from *Texas Trails Magazine*," Tyler said cooly. "They're doing an article about the area and taking photos."

"Wonderful!" she practically shouted. "About time some other parts of Texas paid attention to us."

"It's a great area, not showcased enough," Dan said.

Dorrie stared at RaeAnne. "Guess Tyler told y'all about how close we are," she had the gall to say.

"We're *not*," Tyler said firmly.

"Oh, c'mon, honey. Don't be shy." Dorrie said as she slid a hand across his shoulder.

"I'm not. Dorrie's a confirmed flirt." Tyler decided to make a joke of it. "She wants to date ten guys at once. She's going for the county record."

Dorrie flushed. "That's an exaggeration."

"C'mon, Dorrie," Clay said. "We all know you're trying to break the record set by Alice Eve."

"I am not!" Her indignant expression was priceless. "Listen, here, you—" she paused, and a cunning look overtook her face. Turning to Dan and Sean, she said "although, with you two, I wouldn't mind a threesome."

RaeAnne made a choking sound.

Kristy gawked at the woman. Dan chuckled, and Sean turned red.

"Sorry, I have a girlfriend back in Dallas," Sean mumbled.

Dan said, "Maybe I'll take you up on that… another time."

"Hmph. Well, so long." Dorrie flounced away.

Clay laughed after she'd left. "What a weirdo."

"Weird, and persistent," Tyler complained.

"She always like that?" Dan asked, amusement on his face.

"Yeah, unfortunately," Tyler said.

"It must get annoying," RaeAnne remarked.

Tyler turned to her. "It is. *Very*." *But if* you *want to fool around...* he couldn't help the thought that sprang to mind.

Of course, he'd never want a threesome. He'd want to keep her to himself.

It hit him like a rock, just how much he wanted to keep her to himself. Only to himself.

As if he was falling...

Shoot.

He was falling for a girl he'd just met.

It wasn't so unbelievable. It had happened to his father.

So... it could happen to him.

"Huh?" Clay asked.

He stared at his brother.

"I just asked you a question." Clay stared at him.

Shit. For a moment he wondered if he'd spoken his thoughts aloud.

"Sorry, I was concentrating on my food," he said. "What did you say?"

"I asked if you were doing any more modeling for them," Clay said.

"No, I'm done. They're taking photos of the countryside and towns around here," Tyler said.

RaeAnne had begun chatting with Kristy across the table. Something about sandals and shoes. Women talk. Tyler concentrated on his food, listening with half an ear to the women and to the discussion of baseball which Sean had brought up again.

But his ears perked up as they were finishing and Clay suggested, "Why don't we all go for a swim at Missy's B&B? It's gonna be pretty hot even when the sun goes down."

Tyler looked at his brother. Clay waggled his eyebrows at him.

Yeah, he'd be pretty hot—hot for RaeAnne.

Hmm… maybe his little brother was actually trying to get him some additional time with RaeAnne.

Which he would like. A lot.

He really liked her. His only fear was, what if she was like Audrey? She didn't *seem* to be a shallow woman like Audrey, but still—he hadn't been a good judge of character where his old girlfriend was concerned. That lady had practically jumped his bones, and when he thought after a few months, that they were getting close on an emotional level, she'd dumped him. Claimed she'd only wanted an affair with a cowboy, but she really wanted a big-shot corporate type.

He'd been hurt. And angry with himself for not seeing the signs of how shallow Audrey really was.

But RaeAnne didn't seem to be that type.

"Sounds like a plan," he agreed, as several others nodded.

RaeAnne hesitated, then said, "A dip in the water would be good."

More than good.

* * *

Back at the B&B, RaeAnne changed into her burgundy one-piece suit, and stepped outside. The sun was just going down and the air was still hot. She pushed her hair back, catching the scent of the citronella candle as she strode over to the pool.

Tyler and Clay had said they were stopping to get their swimsuits but would be there shortly. Kristy had declared she was tired and was turning in, but Dan and Sean were already in the pool.

RaeAnne felt sticky as she dropped her towel on a chaise and walked to the pool. Stepping in, her mind turned back to their dinner conversation.

She had a feeling Tyler would be persistent and ask her again about her family.

Sighing, she swam across the pool. Her friends already knew her family history. All about her scattered childhood and her mother's four marriages.

The water eased her worries as she floated.

Besides her mother's inconsistent record, she didn't have a great track record herself. She'd dated casually, and then —she'd met Ben Camp.

She did *not* want to think about Ben. Firmly, she pushed aside his image and thoughts of him.

Her biggest failure.

She did a couple of laps, then floated again. The night sky was now dark, with stars twinkling above her. The air remained hot, but the pool was delightful. Sean and Dan were sitting on the chaises, talking.

As she took in the majestic sky, she heard Tyler and Clay approaching.

Tyler looked—well, handsome She couldn't help the thought. His broad shoulders, slim hips, masculine appeal—even in the semi-dark. Maybe the semi-dark made him even more appealing. It was, after all, a romantic setting under a starry Texas night sky.

She began treading water.

She shouldn't be thinking this way. She'd had enough of handsome Texas cowboys after Ben.

"Hey," Tyler said.

"Hi," she murmured.

"How did you like dinner?" he asked.

"That was one of the best cheeseburgers I've ever had," she answered.

"Good night, folks," Dan called, getting up.

"It's early," Clay protested. "Are you a morning person like Kristy?"

RaeAnne guessed Clay had hoped to talk more sports with Dan. Or maybe about the grilling competitions he enjoyed. Dan had been asking him a lot of questions about them.

"I want to go over my photos one more time, and watch a little TV," Dan said. "But I'm sure I'll see you again, Clay. Goodnight, all." He disappeared inside.

Sean dove into the water and Clay followed. They stayed in the deep end, and RaeAnne wondered if Tyler had asked his brother to give them a little privacy.

"If you feel like dessert, my sister still has some of that blueberry pie left," Tyler said.

"I might have some later," she told him. Everyone had been too stuffed from dinner to eat dessert, but the thought of a snack later was tempting. Almost as tempting as the guy right in front of her.

"Okay. Maybe I'll join you. So what do you think of the canyon?" he asked her abruptly.

"I like it," she said slowly. "It's hot, but there's always air-conditioning. And this—" she indicated the sky—"is so gorgeous. Without the city lights of Dallas, you can really see the stars."

"There's Saturn." He pointed to a light that looked like a particularly bright star.

"Do you know a lot about astronomy?" she asked, turning to face him in the water.

"Some." He shrugged. "You learn a little bit when you're camping out. And sometimes you need to figure out directions when you're riding. It's easy to get lost in Texas."

"I can imagine," she said.

Clay and Sean left the pool and walked inside the house. Clay said something about baseball as they slid the glass door shut with a click.

There was a beat of silence, and then he asked, "So now that we're almost alone together—can you tell me about your family?"

"I guess so." She lowered her voice.

"You already know my father died when I was five and my sister was two."

"That must've been tough."

"My mother packed me and Mary Beth up and brought us to Houston, which was where she was from. We spent the next few years there. My mother married again a year after my father passed—George . And she had my half-brother, Jimmy."

Tyler appeared to be waiting, as if he sensed there was a lot more to her story.

"George drank a lot, though. So when Jimmy was four—I was twelve and Mary Beth was nine—she divorced George. Then she met Carl. She married him almost right away, and we all moved to Boston, where he was from."

"Boston?" he asked, astounded. "That's far away. And cold."

"Yes, but it's a really interesting city." RaeAnne paused. "We lived in the city for a few months, then in one of the suburbs. It was very cold. But, like I said, an interesting city."

"How long did you live there?" he asked.

"Until I was about sixteen. Then my mother discovered he'd been having affairs—more than one, so she packed us up again and we headed back to Bellaire near Houston. She was an X-ray technician so she had no problem finding work," Rae Anne added. She swam to the side of the pool, then climbed out and sat on the edge.

Tyler swam behind her, and pulled himself up next to her. "That must have been tough, moving around so much."

"Yeah, plus having different fathers."

"Did you miss the canyon?"

"Sometimes. I missed seeing my grandparents when we lived far away. Now I only have one grandmother left. And I missed the stability many of my friends had, growing up and staying in one place— or at least not living in so many."

"So what happened after Houston?" His expression was empathetic, and RaeAnne felt herself grow warm inside. It was—he seemed to really care.

"After high school I went to U of New Mexico, which I really loved. During my freshman year my mother got married again, to a man named Frank. So far, that marriage is working out." She shrugged. "But who knows how long it will last. I'm twenty-six, and I've had three stepfathers." She sighed. "MaryBeth is twenty-three and she's a high school history teacher near Houston. Jimmy's headed to U of Houston in the fall. He's planning to study business."

"You haven't had it easy," Tyler observed. "You deserve your own happy ending."

"Thank you," she murmured. She wished she could believe in happy-ever-afters.

"I mean it," he said. "You've been through a lot of changes. But you appear to have weathered them." He touched her hand gently. "It must have been a kind of lonely childhood, what with moving so much and changing families."

Right now, she didn't feel lost or lonely. She felt very much alive. The air buzzed, and not just from the nocturnal insects. It seemed the air vibrated simply form Tyler's presence.

And she could feel the answering vibrations thrumming within herself.

Why had she blurted out her whole family history? Tyler was probably going to think she needed a shrink after hearing her talk about her family. She hadn't meant to tell him so many details about her mother's multiple marriages. But he'd seemed sympathetic, and somehow everything just started to leak out. And once it did, it was as if she couldn't stop.

Four marriages. RaeAnne had realized years ago that her mother obviously didn't want to be without a man. Unfortunately, the men she'd chosen hadn't had the best characters, either. A drunk, a cheat—and who knows how things might end up with Frank? They'd been married over six years, which was a record for her mother, but still—who knew if it would last? Probably not. Her mother certainly didn't have good judgment.

He slid a little closer on the pool's edge,splashing his feet in the pool. "Tell me about where you live in Dallas."

Maybe he was trying to change the topic to a more neutral one.

"It's a garden apartment. I live on the first floor. I have a livingroom, kitchen and dining area, a bedroom and bath, and a small space off the livingroom I use as a home office."

"Sounds nice."

"And you? Tell me about your house."

"I had it built on a couple of acres adjoining the ranch my folks, my brother and I own and work on," he said. "Clay is going to build a home soon on an adjoining acre. My home is a ranch. Three bedrooms, two baths, living room, kitchen and dining room. I have a basement I haven't finished yet and a garage. Right now I use one of the bedrooms as a home office too, and the third is a guestroom."

"That sounds really nice," she said. "I'd love a house and a yard for a dog, but I'm not home enough to have dogs. And I can't afford a house right now. Magazines don't pay all that well, although I do love my job."

"I didn't know that," he said, giving her a sympathetic look.

"In the meantime, I'm working on a freelance project. If it succeeds, I'll have a lot of satisfaction— and maybe make some extra bucks."

"What is it?" he asked.

"Long story," she said. She really didn't want to share all her secrets with him. "Uhmm… I think I'll get out now. I'm nice and cool."

Actually, being near him kept her anything but cool. Even by the pool, she could feel heat wafting from him. Heat… and masculine appeal. It was too tempting.

Before she did something foolish. Like slide over towards him and wrap herself around that rock-hard body…

And she'd already spilled too many personal details about herself, so … she stood up.

Tyler followed suit.

"Guess I'll get out, too," he said.

He looked like some god of the sea, all fit and hard, a swimmer's body. All he needed was a triton and he'd look exactly like the god Neptune. Or like a merman. She'd read a romance novel about one recently. Either way, Tyler looked incredible. Incredibly yummy.

She sighed, and grabbed her towel. She did not need another good-looking, hot cowboy to tangle with. One experience like that had been more than enough.

She toweled her hair as Tyler grabbed his own towel.

"I'd like to hear about your project sometime," he said in an encouraging voice.

"I'll tell you another time," she said, forcing herself to sound light. "You've already heard enough about my history for the next month."

"I haven't heard nearly enough," he said solemnly.

She swallowed. How could he seem so nice?

Maybe because he is, a little voice in her head whispered.

"Let's have some pie," she said, pulling on the white cover-up she'd brought with her. She felt too bare, too vulnerable, in just her swimsuit.

They made their way to the kitchen where Sean and Clay were still talking. There was very little pie left, and she let Tyler take the biggest piece. The four of them spoke about where they'd gone to school, as they ate.

"That was delicious," she said as she finished her portion.

"Yeah." Sean stood up. "I'm going to call my girlfriend. Good night everyone." He left the room.

RaeAnne yawned. "I'm tired. I guess I'll see you guys soon."

"How about Friday? We can go to the Sugar Shack. It's the best honky tonk around here," suggested Tyler.

RaeAnne hesitated.

"You can come, too," Tyler told his brother. "Bring a friend."

Was this a double date? Maybe he was trying to make her feel more at ease with a group. "It'll be fun," Clay urged. "How long has it been since you went to one?"

"Not for years," she admitted.

"Then you have to go," Tyler smiled. "Please?"

"Everyone from the magazine can come, too," Clay cajoled.

It could be fun. "Okay," she agreed. She was looking forward to it.

"I—I promised to call my sister," she improvised hastily. She needed to escape, to sit quietly and think about the day. And Tyler. And seeing him again. "Goodnight."

Tyler stood. "I'll walk you out of the kitchen," he offered.

She raised her eyebrows. "Like walking me to my door?"

He grinned. "That too, if you want."

"No, thanks. Goodnight." She beat a hasty retreat.

As she walked down the hall, she heard Clay tease his brother. "Looks like you struck out there, bro."

She couldn't hear Tyler's low response.

She hurried up to her room. Kristy was probably fast asleep, so she'd have the bathroom they shared to herself.

Music floated down from the third floor. Dan liked to listen to music while he edited. She could hear Sean's voice, muffled, from the first room she passed. The rooms at the front of the house—Missy and her daughters' rooms—were dark. They were probably fast asleep. And Kristy's room, near hers, was likewise dark under the door. The hall lights were dim, just light enough for her to see where she was walking, but dark enough not to disturb anyone sleeping.

She took another, quick shower, then got into bed with a historical romance novel. Time to indulge in some real cowboy tales of the Old West.

Her phone buzzed, and she saw it was her sister Mary Beth.

She discussed the day—and her attraction to Tyler—with her sister. Mary Beth, who had dated a lot of guys, had simple advice for RaeAnne. "Go out and have a good time!"

"What if Tyler is like Ben?" RaeAnne asked.

"So, if you're just having fun, does it matter?" Mary Beth challenged her. "Just enjoy the time you spend with him. That's all."

She wondered abiout her sister's advice.

RaeAnne pulled the comforter up, enjoying the cool air of the air conditioner. She opened the book to read.

But she kept picturing the hero as looking exactly like Tyler Quimby.

CHAPTER VI

Tyler was up at dawn, and readied himself for a long day. It hadn't helped that his dreams last night were punctuated by images of RaeAnne Tilton and her sexy body beside his on Thunder.

As predicted, the sunny skies had turned gray. They were in for heavy rains, which, as usual in the summer, they badly needed. It also meant that it would be all hands on deck, stacking hay bales in the barns to keep them dry.

He gulped down his coffee, grabbed a roll, then headed out.

His dad was outside along with two of their hands when he arrived. "Hey," Tyler called out as Clay pulled up in his truck.

Tyler expected more good-natured teasing from his brother about his crush, as Clay called it, on RaeAnne.

But it wasn't a crush. He already knew it went deeper than that. Deeper than his feelings for Audrey had been.

But Clay was all business this morning, for a change. They got to work along with the rest of the ranch's employees, breaking up into groups.

He had no time for photos today, but he missed the interaction with RaeAnne.

An hour later, his mother was there with extra coffee and some donuts for everyone. Soon afterwards, he took a break and noticed that, despite the cloudy weather, Dan and Sean were outside, photographing the men at work.

"Hi," Dan said. "Hope you don't mind, I'd like to get some realistic shots of what goes on with a working ranch. And some landscapes, too, with this different lighting." He glanced at the overcast sky. "I won't interrupt you guys."

"No problem. Help yourself to coffee," he told the two.

The morning was long and hard, with lots of lifting. When they broke to eat lunch, he was grateful for the sandwiches his mother and sister had packed, and for the cake Manny's wife had made.

He didn't see RaeAnne or Kristy until after lunch. They drove in, alighted from the truck, and Kristy took out two cameras.

RaeAnne waved but didn't interrupt him as he hauled a bale out of Xavier's truck and passed it to Bobby, another of their cowhands.

He couldn't wait until Friday.

* * *

RaeAnne had spent the morning with Kristy, taking some of the photos Dan wanted of the town of Claude to enhance the article. Dan was taking the unexpected opportunity to photograph the ranch in the dimmer light of the cloudy day, as well as getting some real working ranch photos.

She loved the town. People stopped to greet each

other, and acted like old friends even when they didn't know her. So many people had stopped and asked if she and Kristy were "those people out from the Dallas magazine." And they'd welcomed her, inviting them to try the shops and even the beauty parlor there.

She and Kristy ducked into a couple of stores. She bought another paperback book and a magazine to read, and Kristy bought some granola bars to keep in her room for a snack.

"You're Celeste Tilton's granddaughter, aren't you?" an older woman in the small general store asked her.

"Yes, how did you know?" RaeAnne asked.

The woman grinned. "I'm Molly Smithson. My grandson Darren works at the Golden Q. He told me you people are doing an article about the Palo Duro canyon and some other places in the panhandle. It'll be good for business, especially for Melissa May's bed and breakfast."

"I hope so," RaeAnne said.

"Besides, you look a lot like your grandmother's sister, did you know that? I was a year behind her in school, but I remember her. Pretty and sweet. She's living in Wyoming now, I hear tell."

"Yes, she is," RaeAnne concurred. "I haven't seen her in years, but I'm on Facebook with her. Do you really think we look alike?" She hadn't noticed. Of course, the last time she'd seen her great aunt Janie she'd been a teenager. She and Mary Beth had been more interested in hanging out with Janie's granddaughter Sue Ellen, who was their age.

"Sue Ellen—the one near your age, I expect-- she's married now, right?"

"Yes," RaeAnne replied. "And they're expecting a baby."

"How wonderful!" Molly Smithson moved over to the register as another customer approached.

"Good to see you back here," a gray-haired, gray bearded man said. "I remember your grandparents well. Me and your granddad used to go fishing together with my cousin Eddie."

Kristy practically rolled her eyes.

But RaeAnne found herself smiling at the older man and chatting with him. She loved the camaraderie among the residents here, and the way everyone seemed to know everyone else, down to their extended—and distant—families.

It wasn't like that at home in Dallas. She only knew a couple of neighbors, and she never socialized with them. She rarely even got together with her friends from work, except for Kristy—and she'd known her from before *Texas Trails Magazine*.

She *liked* the coziness here. While her mother used to say disparaging things about this area—how there was no excitement like there was in Houston, how she didn't like people knowing her business, that it could get boring here especially during the winters—RaeAnne could see the charm of the town.

They paid for their purchases, then wandered around. They popped into a shoe store that was having a tremendous sale on boots—and each splurged on a pair. RaeAnne loved the tan boots trimmed with blue that she bought at an excellent price.

They stopped to have lunch at a little café. Then they drove out to the two sites they'd found from *The Cattle Drive* episodes. Kristy had photographed them again, now with the gray-tinted light of the cloudy sky. They'd finished by two, and returned to the Golden Q.

Here, she found all the ranch hands busy. They were bringing in bales of hay and stacking them in the barn. It looked like all the hands were working together in precision.

She couldn't help admiring Tyler's smooth movements, his muscles bunching as he worked, his body very appealing. She might not want any involvements with another cowboy, but she could objectively admire a good-looking one when she saw him.

Tyler seemed unaware that she was watching him, and she was grateful for that. She certainly didn't want to appear like a lovesick woman hungering for a handsome cowboy.

She headed over to talk to Sean. He told her Dan had finished and had gone back to the B&B to edit the photos. He was just sticking around to get a few more.

Kristy joined him, and RaeAnne left them because she wanted to observe the cowboys working. But she knew not to interrupt them as the dark clouds continued to roll over the canyon. She'd speak to them tomorrow and ask her questions when they weren't so busy. She had to admire their dedication and work ethic. These were men who did their jobs with enthusiasm and dedication.

Sean and Kristy returned and loaded up their cameras into RaeAnne's car. As they were doing so, some rain hit her face.

She hadn't realized she was so warm until the cooling drops misted over her. Someone yelled about the rain starting, and the cowboys seemed to double their efforts.

"Another ten minutes and we should be finished!" Tyler yelled.

"Maybe we should help," RaeAnne told her friends. Sean and Kristy nodded, and they approached Tyler.

"We can help," RaeAnne offered.

"Much obliged." He indicated the front of the line where the rest of the guys were taking the hay off the last two trucks.

Much obliged.

A little thrill moved through RaeAnne. She'd always loved that expression, ever since she'd watched the old western shows with her dad. Hearing Tyler say it in his deep voice caused an unexpected reaction inside her. Warmth, like whiskey gliding down her throat.

She smiled.

A guy named Rafe handed the hay to Sean, who handed it to her and Kristy, and then they passed it on to several more ranch hands before being stacked by Clay and Tyler. Concentrating on just moving the hay along smoothly, like an assembly line, she was surprised when Clay announced "this is the last one!"

"Whew," someone down the line said.

The rain was still sparse and misty, but the dark clouds promised heavier rain to come. The group broke up, several finishing something in the barn, a few going over to the horse barn to take care of the horses, and the remaining men calling goodbyes as they got into their trucks and left.

Tyler approached RaeAnne, Sean and Kristy. "Thanks, guys," he said warmly.

As he stood next to RaeAnne, she could see the

weariness on his face and the sweat on his brow. He took off his bandana and wiped his face.

"No problem," she answered, and Sean and Kristy murmured "you're welcome."

"I'll see you tomorrow?" he asked.

"Yes," she answered. Another thrill shimmied up her spine. Tomorrow, they'd be taking photos elsewhere, but Friday night they'd all be heading to the honky tonk.

She gave Sean and Kristy a lift back to the B&B.

"They really need the rain," Sean remarked as RaeAnne started the engine.

"I know," she agreed. "It's hot and dusty here in the summer."

By the time they got back to the B&B, the rain was coming down more steadily.

For the remainder of the afternoon, RaeAnne worked on notes for the article for *Texas Trails*. Then, with a half hour before supper, she turned to the notes for her book and worked on those. She was concentrating so deeply that Kristy had to call her twice from the doorway before she realized it was time to eat.

The evening was quiet. After supper she showered, relaxed and read. When she snapped off the light and pulled the comforter up, she could hear rain pinging against the windows and the house. It was a nice, comforting sound. She sighed, and drifted off to sleep.

* * *

The following day RaeAnne was working with Kristy, Dan and Sean on the article. They were taking photos of Palo Duro canyon, and then another B&B nearby, plus a few more of Missy's B&B.

The rain had stopped during the night, but left the air cooler and refreshingly clear and with much less of the pervasive dust she was getting used to. They were more comfortable while working.

She didn't see the Golden Q and found she was missing Tyler, and his friendly face.

When they returned to the B&B, Sean headed out to visit his girlfriend and wouldn't be back until Sunday night, he told RaeAnne. Dan packed up his jeep to visit a nearby cousin and also wouldn't be back until Sunday.

Kristy's boyfriend Billy was due in around supper time and he was spending the weekend with her. They'd agreed to go to the honky tonk with RaeAnne and some of the ranch hands.

RaeAnne let Kristy use their shared bathroom first to shower, then got in herself. For the evening, she dressed in a denim skirt, her old but comfortable brown boots, and a frilly peach-colored top. She added gold hoop earrings and a peach and brown necklace.

She ate dinner with Kristy and Billy. After taking some time to read and relax alone in her room, she knocked on the door of Kristy's room and announced it was time to leave. She'd offered to drive since Billy had driven hours to get there.

It didn't take long to get to The Sugar Shack, the most popular honky tonk around here, according to Tyler. They were surprised by the candy-pink color of the shack. Once inside, she was struck by not just the loud music, but by the jovial atmosphere. Even at a quarter past eight, people were enjoying themselves.

69

"RaeAnne!"

Tyler looked yummier than ever. His dark hair glinted with gold highlights in the overhead lights. Close up, she could smell the fresh, masculine scent of his aftershave. He wore snug-fitting faded jeans, dark boots, and a forest green T-shirt.

Someone bumped into her, sending her forward, almost into his arms. His hands shot out and gripped her, keeping her from falling.

"Whoa, there, buddy." He chastised the man who had nearly toppled her.

"Sorry." The man slurred the word. Looked like the man had already had quite a bit to drink. "Sorry, honey." He gave RaeAnne a lopsided smile.

"Thanks," she said to Tyler.

He didn't let her go immediately, but held here there, steadying her. The heat of his hands on her arms warmed her. His grip was strong but not tight. Standing so close, she inhaled the scent of clean and fresh shampoo as well as his aftershave.

"You okay?" he asked.

"Yes." *No*. Not quite. She was rapidly falling under his spell and didn't even want to stop it.

She stepped back, putting a little distance between them. "Anyone else here from the ranch?" she asked.

"Yeah. Clay, and Rafe, and Xavier." He indicated them, standing by the bar. "Let me buy you and your friends a drink." he offered.

"Okay." She heard the breathless note in her voice.

Kristy introduced her boyfriend and the two shook hands as the Billy Ray Cyrus song that had been blaring over the loudspeakers ended and the band in the corner began warming up.

"What would you like to drink?" Tyler's breath fanned her cheek. "They serve a great craft beer here that's made locally."

"That sounds good," she answered.

Kristy and Billy opted for the beer, too, and Tyler ordered them a round, insisting on paying. Once they sat down at a long table and were joined by his brother and friends, they talked about the canyon and the hot weather they'd been having.

"We really needed that rain," Clay said, as a young woman brought over their drinks.

"Yeah, and we could use some more," Rafe said. He smiled at the woman serving them. "So, Sheila, honey, when are you gonna go out with me?"

"When pigs fly,." She said spiritedly, and laughed as she set down the last beer with a clink.

She left the table, and Rafe sighed.

"C'mon, Rafe, you know her heart's set on someone else." Xavier glanced at Tyler.

So the cute waitress had a thing for Tyler. RaeAnne wasn't surprised, but the burst of jealousy that sped through her *did* surprise her. A lot. Just because he had flirted with her, RaeAnne, didn't mean he felt more than a liking for her.

But she was afraid she was developing feelings for him. Strong ones.

She bent her head so no one could see her expression, unwilling for anyone to guess her thoughts. Thoughts that Tyler meant something more to her than an acquaintance.

She sipped her drink. The beer was cool and better-tasting than she'd expected.

"Like it?" Tyler asked.

71

"Better than I expected," she said.

"Yeah, this is good." Billy declared, scraping his seat forward so he could get closer to Kristy on his other side.

RaeAnne took another sip. She hadn't expected a craft beer from an unknown brewery to be so good. In fact, she was finding the canyon to be surprising in several ways. The bar, while being boisterous, still had a down-home feel. The people were genuinely friendly—much friendlier than the Dallas city crowd she was used to. And the food and drink she'd had while here could rival Dallas's eateries.

A big man approached, interrupting her thoughts.

"This is Tiny." Tyler introduced him. "The owner here."

RaeAnne, Kristy and Billy greeted him, and he asked a few questions of them. Apparently he'd already heard that they'd come up from Dallas for the magazine article. He wanted to know when it was coming out and what was being featured.

"You can take some pictures here if you'd like," he offered,.

"We just might mention this place in the article," RaeAnne told him. It would be a good idea. She could add it to her sidebar of "More places to go" for the article.

"Let me know if you want to take photos!" he said happily.

Kristy volunteered to take a few shots, and followed him back to the bar.

Tyler slid closer. "How about a dance?"

Excitement shot through her. Dancing with the best looking cowboy there? A guy who seemed nice as well? She might be cautious around cowboys—but she did love to dance.

"Yes."

He pulled her onto the dance floor near Xavier and a blonde

RaeAnne and Tyler were soon moving, around, dancing in a free-style way to the music. More people joined them on the dance floor as she moved her body in time to the beat.

At one point he reached out and, grabbing her hand, twirled her around.

She caught on, and spun under his arm, coming up closer to him.

His hand snagged her by the waist and he pulled her closer. They stepped around some other couples, whirling.

The song ended. She smiled up at him, invigorated and enjoying herself thoroughly.

"I bet you didn't think I could dance," Tyler said, his voice teasing.

"No, I didn't," she admitted. "So many men aren't good at dancing. But you're a good dancer."

"So are you," he said, his gaze lingering on her.

The band began a slower tune, "*Hearts Afire,*" by Earth, Wind and Fire.

Tyler pulled her close. "This is my favorite kind of music." He tightened his hand on hers.

She smelled his woodsy aftershave as he bent close, pulling her tighter against his lean frame. With her hand on his shoulder and her face pressed into the crook of his neck, she felt amazingly protected and cared for. It was a surprisingly good feeling.

She melted into him as the music poured sweetly around them.

The lead singer crooned

Tyler's hand tightened on hers. And she didn't mind, not one little bit.

He began softly singing into her ear, echoing the words of the song.

Surprised that he knew the words, she looked up. His eyes gleamed in the lights from above, and he smiled as he matched the singer, word-for-word, but in a much softer voice, meant for her ears alone.

She shivered, delight and longing moving through her like a stream through a parched canyon.

"Like the music, darlin'?" he whispered.

"Yes. And I like dancing with you."

His smile grew wider. "Me too, darlin'. Me too." He pulled her in closer.

Dancing slowly in his arms was heaven.

She knew she shouldn't feel that way.

But she couldn't help it. This handsome cowboy who she'd been stuck with was full of surprises. He was genuine, and courteous, and caring--everything a man should be.

And she was afraid she was falling for him.

That thought startled her. She didn't want another broken heart. She started to pull away, but he tightened his grip.

"Stay here, RaeAnne."

She pulled back to look at him.

"Shh," he said. "Just relax, and enjoy the dance. With me."

She tried to. She tried to focus on the moment, the fact that she was in his arms, and it felt like they were in a little canyon all their own, without a throng of people surrounding them. At least, while the dance lasted.

She concentrated on feeling her body brush against his, feeling the warmth radiating from him, inhaling his clean, masculine scent. His chest flexed as he breathed, the shallow breaths stirring her hair.

But the music ended sooner than she wanted, and reality returned. She became aware of the crowd around them, the noise of bottles clinking and people talking.

He held onto her hand for a moment. "That was nice. More than nice," he added.

"Hmm hmm," she said, extricating her hand from his, then led the way back to their table. Clay was grinning at them as she slid into her seat. Kristy and Billy were still on the dance floor, but Xavier was there, and gave them both an appraising look.

She reached for the beer and drank the remainder of it, hoping to look innocent, a woman enjoying herself. Not like a woman who was enamored with a man.

She couldn't think of anything to say, so she sat there, gripping her beer.

She wanted to dance with Tyler again—and, yet... She didn't want to. She didn't want him to think she was falling for his good looks or masculine cowboy persona—

"Nice dancing," Xavier remarked.

The others were returning to their table, and RaeAnne turned to Kristy in relief. Now she could speak with her friend insytead of simply concentrating on Tyler."The band is good." She tried to sound like she was merely an enthusiastic listener.

Not as if something was happening between her and Tyler.

The place was growing more crowded, and

RaeAnne picked up a napkin, fanning herself. The breeze she created barely cooled her warm cheeks.

"Hot?" asked Tyler.

You have no idea, she thought. Out loud, she answered, "Yes. It's pretty crowded in here." She fanned herself some more.

He stood up and extended his hand. "C'mon. Let's take a walk outside."

She hesitated.

He grinned. "I won't bite. Let's just go out and cool off for a few minutes."

She let him pull her to her feet and lead the way out of a side door.

Although it was a typical warm Texas summer night, the temperature outside the bar was cooler than inside with the bodies packed together--even with the Sugar Shack's air-conditioner blowing.

He guided her to a picnic table yards away, by a tree.

She glanced up. The sky was dark, with a crescent moon suspended against the velvety darkness, highlighted by stars. She took another breath, smelling sweet flowers she didn't recognize.

"It is beautiful here," she said. "In Dallas, there's too much ambient light to really appreciate the moon and stars."

"Or to appreciate a beautiful woman." He sat on a bench and pulled her onto his lap.

She was conscious immediately of the ridge in his jeans. He was hard.

For her.

Before she could say a word, he threaded his fingers through her hair. "Your hair is beautiful, so silky." He brought her face down to his.

His lips pressed against hers, and a firestorm started deep within her. Flames licked her everywhere, from her lips to her throat to her breasts. And down, down, to that spot between her thighs where she was suddenly aching.

"RaeAnne."Her name sounded like a prayer. He swooped in to kiss her forehead, her cheeks, and her chin before returning to capture her mouth. His scent wrapped around her, just as his arms tightened around her waist.

"Mmm… Tyler…" was all she could whisper as his kiss ignited her.

His lips claimed hers, hungrily demanding. And then his tongue swept inside her mouth, tangling with hers, creating a dance of seduction with every thrust and parry. His kiss was hot—so hot—and she could taste a combination of beer and mint. She sighed against his lips, and found herself matching his eager kiss just as enthusiastically.

"RaeAnne…" he whispered again, then tangled with her tongue in a sensuous dance.

His hand skimmed her side. Then it moved, and clasped her breast.

His touch ignited her further. Any other man who'd touched her there had been a fumbling idiot, she decided, as Tyler's touch was both deft and light. He smoothed his hand over her breast, and her nipple hardened in response. He touched her again there, and she thought she'd melt with desire.

He let go of her lips, but his hand continued to press against her breast, setting off a storm of desire deep within her body.

"RaeAnne," he whispered. "I want you… so

badly… I can hardly think." He fingers slipped under her top, and grazed her nipple through her bra.

Her nipples tightened instantly. And something heated deep inside her, heated to the point of fire.

"I—" She was at a loss for words. She wanted him, too. How crazy was that? She hadn't had a whole lot of experience. A couple of boyfriends in college. And then Ben.

She would *not* think of Ben. Not with Tyler's hand kneading her, making her melt into him, with his kisses wiping out almost every coherent thought.

Then she couldn't think at all.

He slid his hand away from her breast and smoothly caressed her stomach. Then he slid it until it was once more stroking her breast, with only the thin lacy material of her bra between his warm hand and her aching breast.

"God, you are so lovely, RaeAnne," he said. And then he pushed up her top further, and bent his head. He swirled his tongue over her nipple right through the lace of her bra.

She gasped from the impact of his lips and tongue. They heated her from her breast right down to the throbbing need between her thighs.

"Tyler," she cried softly.

"Do you like that, darlin'?" He licked her again.

"I—oh!" She leaned into his mouth.

He gave her more, this time pulling on her nipple with his lips, tugging lightly but, God, did it feel good.

She hadn't realized his hand had moved beneath her skirt until she felt it slide up her thigh, heat trailing where he touched her skin.

He was getting close to exactly where she wanted

him to touch her.

She scooted closer, murmuring something—probably begging for him to touch her there. She could feel the hard ridge of his manhood pressing into her behind, and his hand crept up, slowly, getting deliciously closer to where she wanted him to touch her intimately.

"RaeAnne," he said, his breath blowing hot against her breast.

"Tyler," she gasped. "Tyler—"

"Whazzup, man?"

The voice close by broke their private session like a sudden downpour of rain on a summer night.

She jumped and Tyler's whole body went rigid.

Surfacing from what seemed an ocean of sensual sensations, she became abruptly aware that she and Tyler were sitting on a picnic bench right outside the Honky Tonk, where anyone could stumble upon them while they were making out.

And someone had. A drunk cowboy. She sat up straight, pulling her top down as Tyler withdrew his hand.

"Havin' a good—*hic*—good time, folks?" The man stumbled toward them.

"Get lost, Syd," Tyler said through a clenched jaw.

"Just want to—want to see if there's any action here," the cowboy said. "And I guess there sure is."

RaeAnne felt her face flame.

Tyler stood up. "You're drunk. Get back inside and have one of your buddies drive you home." His hands fisted at his sides.

"Tyler? That... that you?" Syd, stumbled again toward them. "Who you got there with ya?"

Tyler moved in front of her. "None of your

business," he bit out. He put his hands on his hips. "Now get inside before I throw you there."

The cowboy muttered something about people being too sensitive, then stumbled back to the door.

Two minutes later, he was inside.

RaeAnne's heart was still hammering as she straightened her clothes, not so much from the interruption, but from the intense session she'd been having.

A session that might have proceeded to get even more intimate—

"I'm sorry," Tyler said. "But I'm sure he doesn't know who you are." He faced her. "I'm not sorry we kissed, just sorry it was outside like this. Next time, darlin', I'll make sure we have privacy." He bent to whisper in her ear as he spoke, his breath warm and sensual.

"I—" she couldn't think of anything to say. "I don't usually make out in public."

"I know, sweetheart. Next time it will be just you and me and no one else around," he whispered, his voice husky with desire.

He smoothed his hands down her shoulders and arms. "Come riding with me tomorrow afternoon?"

"I-I'd like that." She still felt almost dizzy from desire.

"Okay, let's meet at the barn at one o'clock, and we'll have the rest of the day to spend together." He kissed her, softer this time, but it still sent a jolt through her system.

"Okay." And she leaned in and kissed him back.

His arms came around her waist and pulled her closer. When he finally pulled back, she wanted to protest. "Darlin', when you kiss me like that, I want to take you to bed and never let you go." His sexy Texas drawl seemed to caress her spine.

She felt herself flush. She took a step back, unwilling to tell him just how much she didn't want him to stop.

He touched her cheek. "C'mon, let's go back inside."

She smoothed her hair. "Everyone's going to know exactly-"

He shook his head. "We'll get right on the dance floor, and everyone will think we've been dancing this whole time."

He led her inside and onto the dance floor as promised. The music had gotten even louder and the place was packed with gyrating bodies. As she went into the motions, RaeAnne guessed that Tyler was right. Everyone who saw them would assume they'd been dancing all along.

If only she could stop thinking of what had just happened!

What had she been thinking? She'd been making out with Tyler like a teenager.

When the music ended, they returned to their table, where only Clay and Rafe were sitting, nursing beers.

"Good band, huh?" Clay asked, and RaeAnne had a feeling that Tyler's brother knew they hadn't been dancing all this time.

Kristy and Billy plopped down across the table.

"Yeah, they're awesome," Billy said.

They ordered another round of beer. Listening to the band, it was difficult to talk. About a half hour later, Kristy asked RaeAnne if she'd mind leaving. "Billy's pretty tired from all the driving he did today," she apologized.

"That's okay," RaeAnne responded. The truth was, she wasn't tired—she was actually too keyed up from the interlude with Tyler—but she could use a little time to herself, to wind down, before bed.

And to think about what had occurred between her and Tyler.

They said their goodbyes to the others.

Tyler caught her hand. "Tomorrow," he whispered.

She nodded. "I'll see you then." She might be having conflicting thoughts about Tyler, but her heart was leaping at the idea of seeing him soon.

She caught Clay's speculative look as she followed Kristy to the door.

* * *

They were all quiet on the way back to the B&B. RaeAnne was thinking about Tyler. She still couldn't believe she'd been making out outside like a teenager.

They let themselves in the front door. As Kristy and Billy walked to the stairs, a shadow from the dark parlor moved toward her.

"RaeAnne? Is that you, honey?"

She gasped. "*Ben*?" What on earth was her former boyfriend doing here?

CHAPTER VII

"What—what are you doing here?" she gasped.

He appeared in the doorway to the living room, the pale light from a hall lamp revealing his brown hair, which looked as if he'd been running his hands through it. His handsome face struck her for the first time as rather weak-looking. He still had a nice body and wide hazel eyes.

"Uh oh," Kristy muttered.

Missy appeared from the kitchen area. "Hi," she said, her voice tired. "Ben checked in a few hours ago. He said…" She waved a hand at him.

"I came to see you. This nice lady, Missy, said I could wait here when I told her I was, well, your boyfriend."

"Boyfriend?" RaeAnne stared at him, astonishment rippling through her. "*Boyfriend*? You haven't been my boyfriend for over a year, Ben. Since *you* broke up with *me*." And broke my heart, she added silently.

"I thought—" Shock registered on Missy's face.

"Ummmm… we'll go upstairs to give you some privacy." Kristy grabbed Billy's hand and pulled him toward the stairs.

"We don't need privacy," RaeAnne declared. She could feel her face growing hot as her shock was rapidly replaced by anger. How dare he come strolling into the B&B where she was staying and imply he was her boyfriend?

Ben reached for her hand.

She snatched it out of reach.

Kristy and Billy clomped up the stairs, whispering. Missy stood awkwardly nearby.

"Please." Ben waved his hand. "Let's sit down, and I'll explain."

Fuming, she narrowed her eyes. "There's nothing to explain," she said flatly.

"Yes, there is." He indicated the parlor. "Let's sit down."

"I'll be in the kitchen if you need anything," Missy said, and retreated hastily.

Reluctantly, RaeAnne followed Ben, her heart hammering with… what? Excitement? No. Dread? Confusion, most likely, she decided as she plopped onto a chair.

He took the sofa, sitting in the corner close to her. He moved his leg so their knees were almost touching.

She moved hers away.

Once, she had dreamed of him coming back to her, declaring how sorry he was. Later, she'd realized he was selfish and untrustworthy. She'd been crazy to fall for him, a good-looking, wealthy cowboy who showed her a good time. It wasn't 'til they'd been going out for a few months that she'd had an inkling of flaws. And he sure had them.

And then there was the night she was waiting for him in his apartment and found the lacy black thong laying on the floor by his bed. A thong that wasn't hers. She didn't care for thongs.

That was the night that she saw his flaws clearly.

He cleared his throat.

"Well?" she prompted, hearing the coldness in her voice. She'd spent a lot of nights—too many—crying for this man.

"Sweetie—"

He stopped, then cajoled, "RaeAnne, I realized last week that I really miss you. We were good together, weren't we?" His voice was soft. "We shouldn't give up on such a good relationship so easily. It's been a tough year without you."

She felt herself burning with anger. "*We* shouldn't give up? I'm not the one who suggested ending our relationship—after I found your other girlfriend's thong! You were the one who felt things weren't good enough, as you so crassly put it. You needed someone who understood you better, who complimented you more, who appreciated you—you blamed *me* for your cheating!" Her voice was escalating, so she paused, not wanting to wake anyone up. "You ended it all," she said tersely.

He did look a little embarrassed. "Well, I've learned my lesson," he said quickly. "I didn't appreciate you enough. So I found out from your boss where you were and got a room here. Of course, I was hoping we could stay together—"

"*What?*" She sprang up. "You have got to be kidding. Get lost, Ben." Then she marched to the stairs and ran up them.

But she was fighting tears—of anger, of betrayal. Did he really think he could waltz back into her life and she would simply welcome him into her bed just like that? What nerve!

Missy came running up behind her. "I'm sorry. I didn't mean to eavesdrop, RaeAnne. But I couldn't help hearing. I had the one room over the garage still available and he registered as a guest—" She looked upset.

"It's not your fault," RaeAnne told her. "Of course, if someone wants to stay here and you have a room, you'd want to fill it. He's—he's an ass." She paused and regarded Missy, waving her hand in frustration. "Goodnight."

"Goodnight," Missy said, but she sounded shaky.

RaeAnne practically ran into her room, turned on the light, shut the door, and locked it.

She leaned against it, listening.

She heard Missy move away.

Downstairs, the door slammed.

She knew the lay-out of Missy's house. The room over the garage had to be accessed from the outside, by the garage.

She sank onto the bed close to tears.

First, she'd felt shock. Then, she thought, a combination of excitement—and anger. With, perhaps, a dash of something else.

She tried to analyze it. Was it attraction? Did she miss him?

No.

She got into her pajamas, then stuck the desk chair under the doorknob. A girl couldn't be too careful.

Then she crawled into bed.

She was tired. It had been a long day, and then she'd spent the night dancing.

And doing other things.

She turned, trying to get comfortable. Her hot and heavy session with Tyler was foremost in her mind, but Ben interrupted her thoughts, too.

It was a while before she fell asleep.

* * *

She slept until nearly ten and woke up refreshed.

Once she showered, RaeAnne went down to breakfast. Kristy and Billy were just finishing up.

"What happened last night?" her friend asked, her voice pitched low.

"I told him to get lost," RaeAnne said. "I'm going to have to talk to Missy about letting him stay here— even if I have to pay for the room myself to keep it occupied. I don't feel comfortable if he's here."

"He checked out ten minutes ago," Kristy said. "He said he had some big gala to go to this evening and was disappointed you didn't want to come."

"He didn't invite me, but I wouldn't have gone anyway," RaeAnne said. She poured some coffee and stirred in sugar and milk.

The aroma was rich and satisfying and hearty. The coffee went smoothly down her throat. "Ahh."

"He left you a note," Kristy said. She handed an envelope to RaeAnne.

RaeAnne ignored it in favor of getting herself waffles and syrup and orange juice. Once she'd had a few bites, she opened the envelope with her finger, conscious that Billy and Kristy were studying her not-too-subtly.

The note was brief. With a glance at the others, she said, "I'll read it."

"Sweetie, I'm heading back to Dallas. There's a big charity ball tonight I must go to. I had hoped you would accompany me, but I guess I can scrounge up someone who'd be glad to go."

Ha, she thought. He's trying to make me jealous. She made a face.

Kristy grimaced. "He's trying to make you jealous."

"Exactly," she agreed. "He continues; 'I know you blame me for our break-up, but you have to admit you were losing interest.' That's not true!" she protested.

"'Anyway, RaeAnne, here's my cell number.' "Please call me so we can discuss getting back together. Yours forever, Ben'. *Mine forever*? He's got to be kidding." Anger laced her voice.

But a little part of her asked, would she really, perhaps, love to lead him around and have him dangling after her? Maybe have a hot affair with him?

No, her mind shot back. Sex with Ben had not been hot—it had been lukewarm. No, the only one she'd want to have a hot affair with was—

She sat back, stunned.

Tyler, her mind whispered in a silky voice.

Kristy and Billy were gaping at her.

My God, had she said something aloud?

She stared at them.

Kristy cleared her throat. "You're flushing, RaeAnne. Does this mean you're thinking of getting back with him?" Her friend knew the whole story about Ben—she'd confided in her when it happened—and obviously thought RaeAnne was out of her mind if she was considering going back to Ben.

"No," she said. "I'm not. If I'm flushing it's with anger and resentment. How dare he think he can just go right back to where we were!"

"You're right. The guy's a prick," Kristy said emphatically.

She grinned at her friends' support. "Truer words were never spoken. Now, I'm going to eat my breakfast."

She dug into her waffle, suddenly feeling relief. She wouldn't see Ben again. He was out of her life.

"Billy and I are going to a rodeo about an hour from here," Kristy said. "Want to come?"

"I have plans to go riding with Tyler," RaeAnne said, and caught the surprise in Kristy's face.

"Well, that sounds like fun," her friend said.

They collected their dishes and put them on the side table, then left. RaeAnne finished her breakfast, feeling relieved that Ben was far away by now.

But his actions—and words—still disturbed her. He had hurt her, thrown her over and now he wanted to stroll back into her life as if nothing happened. Like she would be glad to see him?

What conceit!

It would serve Ben right if she flirted with him, had an affair with him, and then broke up with him.

She poured another cup of coffee, and went to look out the window.

The view was pretty. There was a small garden in the back, and right now Missy and her daughters were watering the flowers.

Deliberately, RaeAnne thought about Tyler.

She couldn't help hearing her sister's advice echoing in her mind—to go out and have fun with a handsome cowboy, to simply have a good time.

Maybe that was exactly what she needed.

She was looking forward to being with him, and riding. She hadn't ridden for at least two years, but, she was sure she'd find her rhythym in the saddle pretty quickly.

Thoughts of being with Tyler again, possibly kissing like they had last night, made her grow warm. All over.

His kisses had been wonderful, addictive, and she'd wanted them to go on and on.

She'd wanted a lot more

Sighing, she gathered up her dishes and mug, placing them on the other table for Missy, and went to her room to decide what to wear.

She settled on worn blue jeans and a comfortable pale green T-shirt. After all, they were just going to ride, and she wanted to be comfortable.

Since it was several hours before she'd agreed to meet Tyler, she spent time calling her best friend Tara and filling her in on what had been going on, including her attraction to Tyler and the surprise visit from Ben.

"I'm afraid I haven't seen the last of Ben," she admitted to her friend.

"You're probably right," Tara agreed. "But don't go back to him!"

"I won't!"

After the call, RaeAnne settled into a comfortable chair to read.

She took a break, thinking about the visit last night by Ben.

She wondered again about having an affair with him, then stomping on his heart. But she couldn't picture herself doing that—or enjoying the affair very much, either.

Revenge, though sweet, was not what she wanted.

Now a hot affair with someone else might be exactly what she needed...

CHAPTER VIII

By twelve forty-five, Tyler was ready and getting the horses saddled.

He'd swung by the liquor store to pick up champagne and he'd packed a basket with it and some snacks. Now he was waiting impatiently for RaeAnne to meet him.

Last night had been unbelievable. He'd made out with her like a horny teenager, barely aware that they were outside where anyone could stumble on them.

In fact, a drunk had done just that.

He sighed, patting Pretty Woman, the horse he'd selected for RaeAnne. She was even-tempered and, since he didn't know how good a rider RaeAnne was, he'd also wanted a horse that was fairly easy to handle.

He'd planned to take her into the heart of the canyon, near his favorite big rock, the one where he used to sit sometimes and dream.

Occasionally, he'd even imagined a woman sitting there by his side.

Instantly, an image of RaeAnne, sitting next to him, popped into his brain. They were leaning against the rock, comfortable and cozy.

He shook his head, and forced himself back to the present.

He'd packed along a blanket for them to stretch out on.

Along with the two condoms he always kept in his wallet—just in case. He guessed RaeAnne wasn't the type to sleep around much, but he was hoping, that with the fierce attraction between them, they might end up in bed together at some point.

Regardless of whether they ended up in bed, he wanted to spend time with her and get to know her better.

He heard a crunch of tires on gravel and gave both horses quick pats before poking his head outside the barn.

RaeAnne pulled her jeep to the side of the parking area and got out.

She looked beautiful. Her lustrous blonde hair was pulled back in a covered elastic band, and she wore a clingy green T-shirt and faded jeans that showed off her slim but curvy figure to perfection. Her beautiful face was smiling as she hopped out of the jeep.

Immediately, a rush of happiness filled him. He was excited to see her.

"Hi," she greeted him.

"Hi." He was struck again by how pretty she was. Her thick hair shone in the early afternoon sun, with almost-red and gold glints highlighting the honey strands. Her kissable lips were smiling in a sincere, enchanting smile that sent waves of longing wrapping around him. Her nose was pert and her wide green eyes were simply beautiful as they gazed at him.

He wanted to scoop her up and kiss her.

He tamped down that impulse, and instead strode over and hugged her.

"I can't wait to go riding with you," he said.

Her smile broadened. "I've been looking forward to it, too."

"I have a special place to show you,"he added

"A special place? I can't wait."

* * *

Tyler helped RaeAnne onto the horse.

His touch was firm but not too tight. Still, waves of heat shimmered around her. She wanted to feel his hands on her, to revel in that electrifying touch of his.

She swallowed as longing bombarded her whole being.

"Where are we going?" she asked.

"To a small canyon right by Palo Duro Canyon," he told her. "We locals call it El Pequeño—the small one."

They started off, and RaeAnne felt relieved when the motions of being on horseback came back to her.

"You're riding fine," Tyler said after a few minutes.

"I was afraid I might have forgotten since it's been a couple of years," she confessed.

He laughed. "It's like swimming. You never forget."

He pointed out some sights to her—a rock that teens painted the names of their latest loves on; a tree that was the source of an infamous hanging in the late 1880s; a house up on a mountainside said to be haunted by the spirit of an Indian who didn't want a house put where he'd died.

"It's all fascinating. I have to make notes later

and put this in my article," she told him as they rode closer to a hill.

Eventually they entered a canyon.

It was not as large as Palo Duro, but it was just as picturesque. Wildflowers bloomed everywhere, and a small stream bisected a corner. A large boulder sat near the edge of the stream beside a huge tree.

"Oh my goodness!" she gasped, pleasure shooting through her. "This is where they filmed the episode "The Sorcerer Meets *The Cattle Drive*."

He looked at her with admiration. "Yes," he said. "*The Cattle Drive* is my father's favorite western series and he recognized the setting right away. It's still one of his favorite episodes in the whole series."

"It was my father's favorite, too." She moved her horse toward the stream. "We used to watch that show all the time."

"Let's camp here," he suggested. "I brought snacks and drinks."

After giving the horses their heads at the stream, they tethered them beneath the tree where they were content to munch on the grass.

They grabbed a blanket and the food out of his saddle bag and spread the blanket on the grass.

In the shade, with a mild breeze blowing, the afternoon temperature was bearable and RaeAnne sat beside Tyler.

"Tell me how you know so much about the show when you watched as a little kid."

"I did watch with my dad, but after he died, I periodically watched it and other westerns too. *The Cattle Drive* and *Cheyenne* were my favorite series. I know that *The Cattle Drive* shot a lot of episodes in

Texas, and several around here. So I decided to write a book about the show, and include information on where some of the episodes were filmed. I'm going to mention it in my article for *Texas Trails*, too."

"You're writing a book." He smiled at her. "That's terrific! I admire anyone who can do that. It must be a lot of work."

"Yes, but I'm enjoying it," she said. "If I can bring to life the areas where the show was filmed as well as other aspects of the show—it's a classic, really—I will have accomplished my purpose."

He withdrew a bottle and plastic flutes.

She caught sight of the label. "Champagne?"

"Why not?" he asked. "I'm celebrating having you to myself for a few hours." He took out cheese and crackers, too, and some fruit. Glancing at her, his smile deepened.

"That's sweet," she said. But it was more than sweet. She could feel something hard inside of her actually melting. Her heart?

He passed her a flute. He raised his. "To a great article in *Texas Trails*. And to your book."

She tipped her plastic to his. "To a great article," she echoed, "and book."

She took a deep breath, and once again smelled the fresh, outdoorsy scent of his aftershave. She lifted the glass to her mouth and sipped.

Bubbles tickled her nose. It was not too dry, and tasted sweet and delicious.

"That's good." She sipped again. She could feel warmth follow the trail of the effervescent liquid.

She looked at Tyler and found he was studying her.

95

He traced a finger along her face. "You're beautiful, you know."

She shook her head. "I'm—"

"You *are,*" he insisted. "Anyone who says you're not is an idiot."

"Oh. Well-thanks."

He paused. "Missy said some guy came to see you last night." He studied her, and she observed his whole body tensing as he sat on the blanket. "What was that all about? Was he really—your boyfriend?"

"*No,*" she said emphatically, taking another sip of champagne. More than a sip, this time. "He was a boyfriend. But—" she stopped

"But?" he asked.

"We broke up over a year ago." She glanced away. "He lied to Missy."

"So why did he come to the B&B?"

She turned her head to regard him. "He wants to get back together," she said dryly.

His entire face grew grim-looking. "Is that what you want?"

"*No,*" she emphasized. "No way."

"What?"

"He hurt me. Broke my heart." she added.

He drank some champagne, then leaned closer. "Why don't you tell me about it?"

"I—" she paused.

"It might help to have a sympathetic ear," he said. His tone was casual, but RaeAnne got the feeling that he was anxious to hear what she had to say. He propped his flute against the tree.

Seeing the concern on his face, she felt something melt inside of her. And—she felt a trust in Tyler. A

96

trust that grew as she stared at him. The story began pouring out of her.

"I met Ben about a year and a half ago." She set down her champagne flute. "My mother's fourth husband—Frank—has a daughter, Lizzie. They were hosting an engagement party for Lizzie and her fiancé at a restaurant. Ben was there. His father is a cousin of Frank's but I hadn't met him before because he travels a lot. Ben and I started talking, and he asked me out."

Tyler poured her some more champagne, handing her the flute. "Go on."

She drank some more. "We began going out every Saturday, then during the week, too. He lived in Dallas also, not too far from me. He was attentive and fun to be with. He took me places I wanted to go. Nice restaurants, the theatre… Anyway, he would do things like bring me flowers and he seemed so romantic. I fell for him." She sighed. Although Ben had treated her well, sex between them had been mediocre.

She was not going to discuss that with Tyler, however.

"And…" Tyler said.

"I began to notice little things. Ben grew up in a wealthy family that had a large ranch. He worked it, but not as hard as you, and not all the time. He wasn't very considerate of others—employees, his family, even his friends. He had a selfish streak."

Tyler nodded.

"Eventually," she continued, "it began to spill over to me. He'd forget to call when he said he would, he'd forget he promised to pick up wine for a birthday party we were going to—that sort of thing. Small things, but they began to add up." She frowned. "It

97

was as if he was done impressing me and went back to his normal, self-centered ways." She sighed. "I let him know how I felt.

"One day," she went on, "I was waiting for him in his apartment and I found—something belonging to another woman." She didn't want to mention the thong specifically. "When I confronted him, he said it was my fault he had another girlfriend, if I had been better to him—" Her voice cracked. Tears filled her eyes. Even now, Ben's words hurt. "I thought I was in love with him, but obviously he didn't feel the same."

"What an asshole!" Tyler exclaimed.

She focused on his face and found he looked angry.

"You deserve better than some guy who's going to put you down. Obviously, he loved just himself, not you."

Loved himself? She gaped at Tyler. "I—I never thought of it quite that way," she said. "I thought he didn't love me, though I was in love with him. I figured I had been fooling myself that he loved me, too."

"A guy like that," he leaned closer, "only loves himself. It has nothing to do with you. He's just not capable of loving anyone else. Period."

She stared at Tyler. He grasped her hand tightly.

"He didn't appreciate the wonderful woman you are," he told her. "You're very special, RaeAnne." His words, spoken more softly now, whispered past her face.

"Thank you," she said.

He touched her face. "You deserve better. A guy who loves you, who will be devoted to you."

She sucked in her breath.

He placed his flute down beside the blanket, then cupped her face in his hands. "Any guy lucky enough to have you for his girlfriend," he whispered, "should be devoted to you and care for you."

Her heart thudded at his words.

She felt the warmth of his fingers, caught the scent of his aftershave before his mouth captured hers.

His kiss was soft, but within seconds it grew harder. More demanding. He pulled her against him and they slid to the blanket, side-by-side.

His tongue swept into her mouth. He tasted of champagne.

She opened her mouth wider, allowing him access, and her tongue tangled with his.

He kissed her hungrily, wide, open-mouthed kisses that became increasingly intense.

"RaeAnne." he whispered. His hand trailed down her side, leaving a trail of fire where he touched her thin T-shirt.

She'd been thinking about kissing Tyler again.

Then she couldn't think, she could only *feel*.

His hand brushed her breast, then stroked it. Her nipples pebbled as something deep inside her roared to life. A fire. A hungry heat.

She murmured an entreaty. She moved her hands to wrap around his neck.

"RaeAnne." He slipped his hand under her T-shirt, moving up until he grasped her breast.

Her bra was thin and lacy, and the heat of his hand burned through it. She gasped at the excitement of his touch.

"Tyler."

99

He pulled her T shirt off and then unclasped her bra. He pushed it aside and caressed her breasts.

"You are *gorgeous*," he said.

He made her feel gorgeous.

"And you—" She gasped as he stroked her breast—"are so… handsome and… masculine." She moved her hands over his shoulders, down his hard stomach, and felt the planes of his chest through his flimsy T-shirt.

He sat up, pulling off his T-shirt, and she got a good look at his abs, his flat stomach and strong shoulders.

Then he was back beside her, kissing and caressing her.

As he touched her, something sweet and hot bubbled up inside her, spilling into every vein, every part of her body. She gasped as he suckled her breast, and it was as if a thread tightened inside her.

"RaeAnne, RaeAnne," he whispered, switching to her other breast. He released the button on her jeans, then, slipped inside and touched her through her lacy panties.

She gasped again from his sensuous touch. He stroked her as more sweet heat poured through her.

"I want to make love to you, darlin'," he whispered. His breath feathered her ear.

"Yes," she murmured. A thought interrupted her dreamy state. "Tyler—I'm not—" she struggled to voice her concern.

"I have protection," he said.

She hugged him closer as he continued to touch, his heated caresses and kisses igniting her. She returned his kisses with fervor, loving the way his tongue danced with hers, the warm pressure of his hands, the whispers of endearment.

He slid her jeans down, and they kicked off their boots. He slid off his boxers, and his manhood hardened. Hard and thick and oh-so-ready.

Sliding down beside her, he smoothed a hand over her, then tugged on her lacy blue panties, until she was as naked as him, the blanket underneath cushioning them softly, the shade of the tree providing privacy.

His hand touched her delicately, in the place she ached so much.

She gasped, his touch creating a burning desire within her, a desire for him. Only him.

"Tyler."

"Yes, RaeAnne, yes," he moaned, and she heard the foil packet tear, then felt him move as he sheathed himself. Then he was at her entrance.

"Please," she pleaded, almost frantic to feel him inside her. She'd never felt such longing, such wanting, with anyone. She was so eager to feel him.

With one thrust, he was inside.

He felt so big, so *right*, so perfect inside her. She gasped again, breathless with the feeling of wonder and completeness she felt with him.

Then he began to thrust, and any remaining thoughts flew out of her head. She felt him, felt his manhood, felt his hands, his tender kisses, him, only him.

And suddenly, the waves swelling inside of her burst, and she shot up to the stars.

"Tyler!" she cried out, as the galaxy twinkled and spun around her.

Her voice shattered the tranquil sounds of nature.

And he was right there with her. He yelled out, a complete sound of immense satisfaction.

The canyon echoed around them with their combined cries of passion.

Slowly, they drifted back to earth.

She couldn't speak. He was pressing down on her, a welcome warmth and weight, and she felt the rapid beat of his heart against her skin.

"RaeAnne," he murmured against her cheek. He kissed her then, long and sweetly and delicious waves swept up her spine.

"That was wonderful," he whispered. "You're wonderful."

"That was spectacular," she agreed. "So are you." She sighed.

They lay entwined together, on their sides, content.

Until a gust of wind touched her skin, and she shivered. The hot air didn't seem as warm now, or maybe it was just the wind cooling off the sheen of sweat on her skin.

He hugged her closer. "I want you to come to my house, and sleep with me tonight." He stroked her lightly on her back. "I want to sleep with you in my arms all night."

"Okay," she agreed, pleased. "But I'll need to go back to Missy's and get some clothes and my toiletries."

"No problem." He propped himself up on his arm, and grinned at her. "I'll even make you dinner. I can grill a steak and potatoes as good as the next cowboy."

She smiled back. He wanted to sleep with her in his arms—it was so romantic.

"If you're hungry now, we can have those cheese and crackers with the rest of the champagne," he said.

She *was* hungry. "I guess great sex makes us hungry."

"You bet." He winked.

They quickly pulled on their clothes, stopping to kiss each other.

Once dressed and sitting on the blanket where they'd made passionate love, she hesitated. Sex with Ben had been a matter-of-fact, quick thing, then he would usually get up and have a snack. Or leave. He didn't touch her much or cuddle afterward.

But, apparently, Tyler liked touching. He kissed her a few times, stroked her cheek, and nibbled at her ear as they snacked on the cheese and crackers and had a little more champagne.

He also produced water, "so you won't accuse me of getting you drunk," he teased.

She smiled. "I won't. I knew what I was doing," she kidded back.

He asked her about the canyon and her book, and she loved that he listened to her answers. Really listened, as if it was important to him. Perhaps it was.

They spoke about the horses, his ranch—and he described his dream of growing the ranch and acquiring champion horses for a stud service. "I love horses," he said, "and I believe there's money to be made, and so does Clay. And we treat our horses well," he finished.

"I can tell," she said. "I haven't been around horses much lately, but yours all look healthy and seem very content and happy."

Roni Denholtz

"Not as happy as me." He bent forward and kissed her again.

They cuddled together for a while, quietly content. RaeAnne could not believe how good she felt with Tyler's arms around her. Protected and secure.

The breeze got gustier and the temperature dropped after a while. He glanced at the sky, and said "I believe we may have rain tonight."

"The weather channel said so," she responded.

"We could use it. I guess we better pack up," he said, reluctance in his voice.

She glanced at her watch. It was already four o'clock.

She helped fold the blanket, then stood on tiptoe to kiss him.

Instantly, his arms surrounded her. He nuzzled her neck. "Hmm…" he whispered, and her insides tightened in her at his suggestive sounds.

She was already looking forward to making love with him again.

* * *

He couldn't remember ever feeling this fantastic.

As they rode their horses slowly back to the ranch, Tyler kept glancing at RaeAnne.

She truly was beautiful. With or without her clothes.

His member throbbed at the reminder.

But more than that, she was a nice, sincere person. Sweet.

And giving. After her first hesitation, she'd been as passionate as he wished.

He liked her. A lot.

Hell, maybe he was even falling in love.

He couldn't help grinning at the thought. It seemed he'd finally found that special someone and had tumbled into love as quickly as his father had.

Audrey seemed like such a distant memory now, he could barely remember her face. Not that he wanted to. He pushed aside thoughts of his ex-girlfirend. He'd tell RaeAnne about her eventually.

He reached out as they rode side by side to touch her hand.

She looked at him, startled, then smiled as their eyes met.

Yup, the love-making had been outstanding. And he couldn't wait for a repeat performance.

When they reached the ranch, she helped him take care of the horses.

"Should we feed them?" she asked.

"It's a little early for their supper," he replied. "We take turns on Saturdays. It's Xavier's turn today to feed the horses—and make sure the barn cats are cared for too."

When they got outside, the sky had become totally overcast, and the damp wind was blowing more forcefully.

"I'll follow you to Missy's," he suggested, "then you can follow me to my house. It's only fifteen minutes from hers."

Once they got to the B&B, RaeAnne ran lightly up the stairs while Tyler lounged in the parlor.

He was too keyed up to thumb through a magazine. Faint conversation and a radio came from the kitchen area.

"I thought I heard someone come in." His sister's voice broke through his dreamy thoughts of RaeAnne.

"Yeah. I'm waiting for RaeAnne," he told his sister. "She went up to get something."

His sister regarded him. "You look like a cat who just found a bowl of cream."

He laughed. "Maybe I feel that way." He leaned forward and pitched his voice low. "I think I'm falling in love with her, Missy."

"Really?" Her eyebrows shot up. "Well, good for you. She does seem awfully nice. Does she love you back?"

He shrugged. "Too early to tell, I'm thinking, but I hope so." He grinned at his sister.

She smiled back, and walking over beside him, patted him on the shoulder. "I hope so too."

RaeAnne must have packed her bag quickly, because, a minute later, she was running down the stairs. "I'm ready." She paused at the door to the parlor. "Hi, Missy."

Tyler watched as his sister took in the colorful fabric duffle bag RaeAnne was holding.

RaeAnne flushed.

He stood up. "I'll take that." He took it when RaeAnne handed it over.

Missy just turned to look at him, and winked.

"See you later," he said to his sister.

"Bye," RaeAnne said, but her voice was kind of faint.

"Bye!" Missy said in a very cheerful tone.

He followed RaeAnne out. "Hey," he said, "you can leave your car here and I'll drive."

She hesitated. "Are you sure?"

"Yes." He grinned. "Any time you want to leave, I'll drive you back." But, hopefully, not too soon.

He saw her relax.

"Okay," she agreed.

The drive was short and cheery. He asked her questions about her magazine, and they listened to the radio. His favorite station was doing an hour of Willie Nelson, and he sat back and enjoyed the music and the company as he drove.

Once at his house, he gave her the tour. Living room, dining room, kitchen, laundry, bathroom, two guest bedrooms—one of which he'd turned into a home office—and the master bedroom with a rather luxurious bath, if he did say so himself.

"This is great!" RaeAnne said. "I love that it's colorful and the rooms are large."

"Missy and my mother helped me decorate," he said, pleased that she liked his home.

He dropped her duffle bag on the king-sized bed in his blue master bedroom, and then went to warm up the grill. RaeAnne volunteered to put together a salad with the vegetables in his fridge, and she made baked potatoes in the microwave while he cooked the steaks outside on the grill.

It was comfortable and homey, working alongside her to set the table. He grabbed a bottle of red wine from his collection and poured them each a glass before they sat down to eat.

The meal turned out pretty good. He asked her about the article on the canyon and also the other places which would be included. Then she asked him about college, and he talked about his years at Texas A & M, studying business. "I knew I wanted the ranching life," he said, sprinkling more salt and pepper on his steak. "But I wanted to learn more about running a business."

"And did you ?" she asked.

"Yes," he replied. "I did. And the college years were fun!"

"I agree," she said with a smile.

He would have liked to take her right to bed, but he didn't want her to think that was the only reason he'd brought her to his house. So he suggested watching a movie. She looked over his DVD collection, and selected "Montana," an old western with Errol Flynn. She had never seen it, and they cuddled up on the couch to watch together. It was nice and cozy.

After the movie, they did go to bed. Love-making was slower this time, but just as powerful. When he thrust into her she cried out, and came immediately. He continued to touch her, holding himself back, straining not to come before she could climax again.

And she did, then a third time, before he couldn't stop himself from peaking too.

Afterward, they lay together, wrapped in a light blanket. The air-conditioner hummed in the background, and rain hit the window musically

Within a few minutes she stretched against him, her beautiful body rubbing his. He instantly grew hard.

"RaeAnne…" he whispered.

This time, she deliberately rubbed against him, her eyes open, her smile teasing and tempting. "Feel something you like, cowboy?" she teased.

He pulled her against him.

"I feel something wonderful, something I want

more of." He dipped his head and kissed her hungrily. She'd gotten him going in record time.

They made love again, savoring each other. And it felt just as good as the first two times they'd made love.

Afterward, they held each other close. The rain pinged steadily on the roof and against the window. It was a soothing sound and in a few minutes, RaeAnne's even breathing joined the other night sounds. She was asleep, clinging to him, her head resting on his shoulder.

It felt wonderful.

As he drifted off to sleep, he couldn't help wondering what it would be like to fall asleep like this every night.

* * *

They made love again in the middle of the night when RaeAnne felt Tyler stirring beside her. And when she awoke in the morning, she felt absolutely terrific.

She'd never made love so many times—three!—in one night.

She gazed at Tyler.

Wrapped in the blanket, bare to his waist, his masculine chest moved slowly with each breath. He looked sexy as sin.

She bent to kiss his shoulder lightly.

"Hmm… that feels great, babe," he whispered. He pulled her against him, and they made love again.

Later, they shared a shower. They ended up making love in the shower, too—a new experience for her. Afterward, laughing, they toweled each other off and kissed for a long time. Finally, they tumbled into bed again and made love once more.

RaeAnne had rarely felt so good—so happy and satisfied. She kept touching him, smiling at him and kissing him, and was gratified when he did the same. She'd found an affection she hadn't expected along with great sex.

Tyler's stomach growled, and when RaeAnne looked at the bedside clock, she saw it was nearly ten AM.

"We slept late," she commented, "at least it's late for you."

"Not so much sleeping." He winked. "And it was well worth it." He grinned again. "C'mon, it's Rafe's turn to do the Sunday morning chores. Let's eat breakfast."

They made pancakes together. Tyler's coffee was a little on the strong side for her taste, but RaeAnne didn't complain. How many cowboys could muddle through making breakfast? Ben certainly hadn't been able to. Breakfast at his place consisted of take-in bagels and pastries or cereals and milk.

"How about if we spend the day together?" Tyler asked as he stirred milk and sugar into his second cup of coffee. "We could ride or, we could go see Clay in that grilling competition and sample some food."

"I've never been to that kind of competition," RaeAnne said. "Sounds like fun!"

The weather had cleared, and last night's rains had lowered the temperature a little, so when they set off it wasn't too hot. The competition was over an hour away, but as she spent time with Tyler in the car, with him reaching over to touch her hand or sending her a sexy smile, the time flew by.

It didn't take them long to find Clay and his friends, who competed as the "Irish Golden Guys."

"Their specialty is the brisket sandwich. The sauce is made with whiskey," Tyler told her.

They sampled the sandwiches and sweet potato fries. They were delicious, and RaeAnne agreed with Tyler that Clay and his friends had a great chance of winning the competition today.

They wandered to different booths, sampling chicken as well, and then ice cream. By the time the winners were announced two hours later RaeAnne was hot and getting a little tired.

They stayed for the announcements, and Clay and his friends came in second place.

"This is a prestigious competition, so taking second place is really good," Tyler told her as they applauded.

They returned to his truck, and then waited in line with other vehicles to exit the parking lot. Finally, they were back on the road, the air-conditioning and bottles of water they'd purchased cooling them off.

"Let's go back to my house," Tyler said, sending her a hungry look.

She smiled and patted his knee. "Sure."

They showered again, then fell into bed and made love.

They'd eaten enough so that they weren't particularly hungry at dinner time. Tyler suggested sandwiches so they ate those and watched a little TV.

By ten o'clock, RaeAnne was growing sleepy, and she yawned.

"You better get me back to Missy's," she said, reluctance in her voice. "I have to get up early tomorrow."

"Me, too." He hugged her. "I'd like to see you tomorrow night but I'm going to a Chamber of Commerce dinner with my dad and Clay."

"That's okay," she told him. She leaned over and kissed him. "There's always the rest of the week."

"Let's have dinner on Tuesday," he suggested.

She agreed, then packed up her duffle and, with a few more hugs and kisses, walked with Tyler out to his truck.

When they arrived at Missy's they shared a few more lingering embraces in the truck, then she kissed him again and hopped out when he opened the door for her.

He followed her, grabbed her and gave her a resounding kiss.

"I'll call you tomorrow," he said, his voice husky and appealing. Even those sweet words caused something hot to coil in her belly.

Or maybe it was his kiss.

"Okay," she said, kissing him in return. "Goodnight."

She lightly ran up the three porch steps, let herself in, then waved at him from the doorway.

He was standing there, smiling at her.

She blew him a kiss then continued upstairs.

Kristy's door was ajar, and RaeAnne could hear her speaking on her phone. Billy must have left, since it sounded like she might be talking to him. "Yes, we should definitely go there next weekend," she was saying. RaeAnne also heard a TV on in Dan's room on the top floor. She could hear sirens and the sounds of police. He was probably watching a crime investigative show.

She let herself into her room and sank down on the bed.

What a weekend!

She'd never had one quite like this.

She'd made love before—sometimes good, sometimes just so-so, like many of her encounters with Ben. But she'd never experienced the mind-blowing, exciting sex she had with Tyler. Not ever before.

Not to mention the romantic moments, the cuddling in bed, the sheer enjoyment and pleasure of the whole weekend.

She sat on her bed, wrapped her arms around her middle and sighed blissfully. It had been extraordinary.

This feeling—it was so wonderful, so sweet and thrilling. Almost like—

She stopped, her mind skidding to a halt.

Almost like being in love.

CHAPTER IX

RaeAnne abruptly sat straight up, rejecting the thought. She wasn't in love, was she? She couldn't be. She had vowed after Ben's betrayal that she wouldn't love again for a long, long time.

Almost like being in love…

Wasn't there a song with that title? her mind asked.

And if you're not in love, what exactly are you feeling?

Damned if she knew.

No, she was just having a fling. A hot—really hot!—affair with a handsome hunk of a cowboy.

She was tired, and tomorrow would be another long day of photos and writing. She stood up and got ready for bed, pushing the worrisome thoughts aside.

But once in bed, with the lights off, she couldn't relax and sleep for a while.

Her mind kept wavering between, *this is almost like being in love* and *no, this is just a fling with a hot cowboy.*

* * *

Monday was a busy day. They were at a location about an hour from the B&B, and RaeAnne was taking notes for the article, while Kristy, Dan and Sean were taking all kinds of photos. The sun was hot and they wrapped up just after noon to go back to the B&B and work in the air-conditioned rooms there. After a quick lunch, she settled down to finish outlining and do a brief draft of her article, while things were fresh in her mind. She heard the others upstairs in Dan's suite, discussing the photos and doing some editing.

Tyler called her around two.

"I wish I didn't have this meeting tonight," he said. "I'd rather spend the evening with you."

"Me too," she told him. "But, maybe it will be a productive meeting. And I have work that will probably stretch into this evening, too."

"Ok, darlin'," he said. "I'll speak to you tomorrow. Let's go out for dinner."

"Sounds good to me," she agreed.

He sent her a smacking kiss through the airwaves, and she said goodbye with a laugh and hung up.

It turned out her work went pretty well, and by the time Missy was serving cold cuts and salads for dinner, RaeAnne was finished with her preliminary work and could spend the rest of the evening relaxing. Dan went upstairs to do more editing after dinner, but Sean and Kristy were done with their work for the day. They all ended up watching an action-adventure movie which only Sean had seen, but declared a good one that he would watch again.

The movie was exciting, and afterwards they scattered, Kristy to call Billy and Sean to get on his computer and speak to his girlfriend. RaeAnne showered, then ensconced herself in her room and called Tara, filling her in on every detail of the weekend.

"Wow," was Tara's response. "Just—wow!"

"Yeah," RaeAnne said. "Can you believe it? Me, having a hot affair with a cowboy? And after what happened with Ben... I must be out of my mind."

"No, you're just having a good ol' time," Tara said. "You should have a fling. You deserve some fun in your life."

"I do," RaeAnne agreed. Fun wasn't something she'd had a lot of since Ben broke up with her.

This weekend had certainly been full of fun, and hot sex...

"You do," Tara repeated.

She heard Tara yawn. "It was a busy day for me at work," her friend said. "I'll call you in a couple of days and you can fill me in on what's happening, okay?"

"Okay," RaeAnne said. "Goodnight."

She got into bed and read for a while, but grew sleepy and turned off the light. Weary, she fell asleep soon afterwards.

And dreamed about Tyler kissing her.

* * *

Tuesday dawned sunny and hot. Texas hot. Meaning, hot as hell.

The night before, Dan had announced that he wanted to go back to the Golden Q ranch for a few more photos—and that they'd go to the other ranch tomorrow. He wanted just a few more photos in a different light and he hadn't photographed the ranch yet in the blazing sun that was predicted for Tuesday.

"Wednesday and Thursday we'll do back-to-back days at the other ranch; Wednesday is supposed to be sunny, but Thursday cloudy, so we'll get a variety of lighting," he finished.

Knowing how important the photos were to the article, RaeAnne agreed to his request.

She stood in the shade now. It was a quarter past ten in the morning, and it was already very hot. Kristy and Sean were taking photos of the barn while Dan was photographing some of the cowboys at work. People—and horses—were drinking water often. The cats had disappeared into shady spots, and the dogs were in his parent's house, where the air-conditioning was keeping them cool., Clay had told RaeAnne. They didn't need the dogs at the moment.

She was making some notes about the cowboys' work when her phone rang. Digging it out of her pocket, she saw it was her editor Penny calling.

"Hi Penny," she greeted her.

"RaeAnne?"

Penny's shaking voice alerted her to the fact that something was wrong.

"Yes, it's me," she answered.

"Oh, RaeAnne—" Was that a sob she heard from Penny?

What on earth could be wrong? Was something wrong with Penny's pregnancy?

"Are you okay?" she asked.

"No—I—that is…" Penny took a breath. "I just heard some awful news."

"What?" Penny's distress was making RaeAnne uneasy. She felt herself tensing up.

"A company just bought out *Texas Trails*!"

117

"What?"

"Yes. A company—Awesome Atlanta Entertainment—just bought us out."

"Awesome Atlanta—what does a company in Atlanta Georgia want with us?" RaeAnne asked.

"I don't know! But the worst thing is—" Penny took a breath—"we're all being let go!"

CHAPTER X

"*What?*" Rae Anne gasped.

"Y-yes. They're taking over and bringing in their own people. We're all history!"

RaeAnne's stomach plummeted to the dusty earth. She couldn't believe it. "They're bringing in people from *Atlanta* to run a Texas magazine?"

"Yes. How stupid is that?" Now Penny sounded like she was getting mad. "What do they know about Texas?"

Unfortunately, RaeAnne knew from other editors that takeovers and changing of hands were not uncommon in the world of magazines and media. Letting go of the staff and supplying a new one was not unheard of either.

She wanted to cry. She wanted to pound her fists on something too. "This is terrible!"

"Yes! They told me we'll all get some kind of severance package, and that it will be more than decent—but who knows? We'll be—we'll be out of jobs!" Penny wailed. "It's awful!"

It was not like her editor to wail.

She gripped her phone tighter. "Oh, Penny, it *is* terrible," she repeated.

Now she heard Penny definitely crying. "I'm—so sorry—to tell you this."

"It's not your fault," RaeAnne said. Her legs wobbled, and she looked for a place to sit down. There was a bench not far from the barn, near a tree, although in the morning it was in the sunlight.

Still, she was feeling chilled, so she walked over to the bench and dropped onto it. The sun on her face actually felt good.

"Why are they bringing in their own people?" RaeAnne asked her boss. "Don't they trust us to keep running the magazine?"

"Apparently not." Penny sniffed. "Lots of entertainment corporations take over others, and sometimes—but not always—they bring in their own people. In this case, that's what they want to do. They came in today and told me in person. Now they're going to tell a few others. They're calling a meeting in ten minutes to tell the rest of the staff who are in the office now, but you guys—and the advertising salespeople— are all out. I don't think they're keeping even one person from our staff." She sniffed again, then RaeAnne heard the sound of Penny blowing her nose.

"Oh, shit." The chill in her gut grew bigger. Even with a severance package, she'd have to find another job soon. And she *liked* working at *Texas Trails*. How was she going to find another job—quickly—that she liked as much?

"Could you tell Dan, Sean, and Kristy?" Penny asked shakily.

The knot in RaeAnne's stomach tightened. "Yes," she agreed reluctantly. *Oh, great. Just great.* She'd have to deliver bad news to her friends.

"These people have their own ideas. They must have been planning this for a while. They said to stop whatever we're working on. Their staff is going to take over next July's issue—the one we're working on now—so they want us to just stop what we're doing."

"They aren't going to run this article?" RaeAnne cried, her stomach lurching. *What the hell*? This was going to be a *big* article for her! One that could get her enough attention to, perhaps, bolster her career, maybe give her the impetus to move up in the company—no chance of that now—or look around for a job as a managing editor.

And it would have been the perfect tie-in to her book about *The Cattle Drive*.

"Oh, *no*!" she exclaimed.

"I know," Penny said. "This would have been a big article for you--and Dan. And it would have tied in nicely to your book—" Penny sniffled.

"Oh, here comes Denise. She's crying too." Their advertising director tended to be a little hyper, but even RaeAnne felt like crying. In fact, she felt a tear roll down her cheek, and wiped it with her fingers. She hadn't been aware that she, too, was in tears.

"I'll call you all later." Penny sniffed, and hung up abruptly.

RaeAnne stared at her phone.

She had to tell her friends.

How on earth was she going to tell them?

She looked up. Kristy and Sean were bent over their cameras, talking. Farther away, Dan was adjusting his camera.

She felt sick to her stomach, but she stood up. There was no sense in putting it off.

121

She strode over to Kristy and Sean.

"Hey, guys," she said, doing her best to sound normal. She was afraid she hadn't succeeded. "I just got a call from Penny. She wants me to speak to you."

"What about?" asked Sean, eyes still on his camera.

Kristy looked at her, and paled. "What's wrong?"

"Uhm… I need to speak to you all." RaeAnne waved to Dan. He didn't seem to be noticing her, so she said to the others, "come with me." And then she moved toward Dan.

As she approached, he looked up. He started to smile, then, as she got closer, his smiled faded. He must have seen something in her face that concerned him.

In the meantime, she heard Sean and Kristy's footsteps following in the dusty path.

"RaeAnne! What is it?" Kristy called out.

She reached Dan. "Penny called. I have to talk to all of you."

"Yeah?" Dan asked.

She moved into the shade of another tree, and waited while Dan, Sean and Kristy were surrounding her.

"I have—bad news." This was going to be more difficult than she'd thought. As she gazed at their faces, full of curiosity, she felt that weird chill in the middle of a hot day crawling through her.

"A company—Awesome Atlanta Entertainment— just bought out *Texas Trails Magazine*." She swallowed. "And, they're taking over. Doing a clean sweep. We're all—being let go." Her voice broke.

"What?" Dan practically shouted.

"Huh?" Sean exclaimed.

Kristy gasped.

"Yes, and it sucks," RaeAnne continued. "It's bad enough they want their own people coming in and running the magazine—but what in hell do people from Atlanta, Georgia, know about Texas?"

Kristy burst into tears.

RaeAnne put an arm around her friend. "Penny says we're all going to be given decent severance packages, so we'll be paid for a while at least."

"That's awful!" Kristy said between sobs. "How could they do this? How could management let them?"

"They must have had a good offer from that company," Dan said, his tone grim.

"It's not fair."

"Shit." Sean's face darkened. "I really liked working here, too."

"What about all this?" Dan asked, waving an arm around their surroundings.

RaeAnne swallowed again. "Penny says we've been ordered to stop working. *Now*."

"Now?" Dan exclaimed.

"Yeah," she replied. "I'm as upset as you are." She felt another tear roll down her cheek. "This article... it would have been a great thing for the magazine, for our readers—and for me career-wise. For all of us, I believe."

"I agree." Dan frowned.

Footsteps crunched on the dirt nearby.

Clay was studying them. "Are you guys okay?" he asked.

"No!" Kristy cried.

"No," RaeAnne echoed.

Dan was still swearing. Sean looked shocked.

123

"What's goin' on?" Clay asked, coming to stand by them.

Briefly, RaeAnne described the situation to him.

Clay's expression became almost as dark as Sean's.

"That sucks!" he exclaimed.

"What am I going to do for a job?" Kristy cried.

RaeAnne hugged her friend. "Well at least we'll be getting some kind of severance package to tide us over until we can find something else." Repeating Penny's words wasn't making her feel better, though.

"But I liked this job!" Kristy cried. "I wanted to stay here!"

"I liked it too," RaeAnne said, her voice low. She was beginning to feel defeat creeping through her. For Kristy's sake, she tried not to cry, sensing that would make her friend worse.

"This just blows," Dan said. "Well, time to pack it in. Most of this stuff belongs to *Texas Trails*, so we'll have to return it." He stomped off toward the rest of his equipment.

"I'm really sorry to hear that," Clay said, his voice ringing with sincerity.

"I feel terrible," Rae Anne said, as Sean sent her a sympathetic glance and then followed Dan.

Kristy disentangled herself from RaeAnne's hold. "I better help put our stuff away." She walked off, her shoulders slumped, still crying a little.

"Anything I—we—can do for you guys?" Clay asked.

RaeAnne shook her head. "I don't think so. I guess we'll gather our stuff and leave the ranch."

She walked toward the others, her clipboard and pen still clutched in her hand.

This was awful. She not only liked her job, but this article could have really gotten her name out there, in the spotlight. And it would have been a wonderful lead-in to her book.

Of course, she knew she might be able to gather her research and sell the article elsewhere, but there were no guarantees she could. She'd also have to pay Dan and the others for their photos. She already had an arrangement with Kristy for her book photos—but this would fall outside that agreement.

She worried, too, about her bottom line. Even with unemployment, she'd have to look for a job and maybe take a less desirable one. She still had to eat and pay rent.

Kristy's family was wealthy. But she'd never go to them for help, RaeAnne suspected. They'd made her life difficult and that's when she'd turned to drinking. Now that she had been sober for a few years—without their help—RaeAnne doubted that her friend would want to ask for a hand-out.

Sighing heavily, she wiped away another tear which had crept down her cheek. As she joined her coworkers, she tried to put on a brave face.

* * *

RaeAnne packed the last of her clothes in her suitcase except for the outfit she planned to wear tomorrow.

It was late afternoon. Dan had collected his things, loaded up his car, and taken off for Dallas already. Sean was planning to leave in the morning, as were RaeAnne and Kristy. Kristy had taken a nap when they'd returned to the B&B, and RaeAnne hadn't wanted to disturb her friend. Wednesday morning would be soon enough to return to their former place of work to clear out their desks and do whatever was necessary.

Her mind had drifted to Tyler, but she didn't call him. What could she say? I think I'm crazy about you, but I have to return to my non-existent job in Dallas?

She heard footsteps outside her room, and then someone rapped on her door.

"RaeAnne?" Tyler's voice echoed in the hall.

Relief poured through her. He was here! She stumbled to the door and opened it.

He'd come. In person. To see her.

"Tyler?"

He pulled her into his arms, stepped with her into the room, then shut the door behind her.

He held her tightly. "I got here as soon as I could. Clay told me."

And just like that, the tears she'd kept at bay for hours began to fall.

"Oh, Tyler—" she said, crying quietly into the crook of his neck. "I—I—"

"Shh," he soothed. "I know this is upsetting but you'll find something else. You're talented and there are other opportunities out there."

She pulled back, and looked at him. He was concerned. *For her*.

"You can use this time to work on your book," he suggested. "And maybe even take some time off."

She shook her head. "I don't know what—what kind of package they're offering yet, but I need money to pay my rent and eat and—"

He stroked one hand down her hair in a soothing gesture. "I'm sure if you really need it, you can get help from your family."

"My mom and her fourth husband?" RaeAnne laughed, and, in the quiet room, it was not a pleasant sound. "They're too busy traveling and taking care of their own needs. You probably have the kind of family who would help, but mine—I can't count on them."

"Really?" He looked surprised.

"Really." She shook her head. "I'm the last thing they're worried about. Oh, I suppose if I went over, they'd give me some cash if I was really broke, but they'd never let me move back in. Not that I would ever want to. They have their own life, and they've made that abundantly clear. And anything they did would come with a lecture, about how I need to—" she stopped. She certainly didn't want to confide in Tyler how her mother was always saying she needed a man. Just because her mother was incapable of living without a man beside her, didn't mean RaeAnne was, too. She'd always told her mother when she made that remark that she *didn't* need—or want—a man. She didn't want to be dependent on anyone.

And she'd never trust her own judgment again. Look how wrong she'd been about Ben! She'd loved him, and he'd broken her heart

No, she was just like her mom. She had poor judgment about men—about people in general, probably—and she'd end up going from one man to another if she slipped into that habit.

It was better to depend only on herself.

"RaeAnne?" Tyler asked, pulling back to study her.

127

"I don't want to depend on my mother or her husband," she told him.

He opened his mouth. Then closed it.

She suspected he wanted to say something more, but was hesitant. Instead, he grabbed her and pulled her close again. "It's all right, darlin'," he said. "Things have a way of working out."

"I wish I could believe that."

"You can," he said, emphatically.

Sean knocked on her door. "RaeAnne, are you ready to go to dinner?'

She looked up at Tyler, pulling back again. "Sean and Kristy and I decided to eat at the diner."

He nodded. "I actually have to finish up some work, too. I just had to see you."

"That was nice of you," she whispered.

"Of course. Listen, I'll come back, let's say around eight?" he asked.

She smiled, although she knew it must look stiff. "Okay. We should be back by then."

"Okay, I'll see you then," he said, and gave her a sound kiss on the lips.

It left her tingling.

* * *

Tyler arrived at ten to eight, at the same time RaeAnne, Kristy and Sean were exiting RaeAnne's car.

"I'm calling Billy," Kristy said, her voice sounding strained, and ran up the steps into the B&B.

RaeAnne turned as Tyler slid out of his car, and forced a smile.

"I'm calling Jill," Sean announced, and followed Kristy into the house.

"Hey," Tyler called out to RaeAnne. He strode over to her.

He wrapped his arms around her. "How are you feeling now?"

"We're all gloomy." She leaned into him.

"I'll cheer you up," he promised.

She looked up at him. He wore an expression of sincerity, and a little ripple of pleasure wove through her. He meant it. He wanted to cheer her up.

"I know you'll try," she murmured.

"I will succeed." He held her tightly.

They stood for a few moments like that, until she sighed and stepped back.

"C'mon," he urged. "Let's go inside."

She let him lead her into the house. She could hear the sounds of Missy and her kids from the kitchen. They went upstairs, where Kristy's door was closed, but she was loudly complaining through it. Passing Sean's door, they could hear him, but his voice was low and the words indistinct.

Tyler opened her door and ushered her inside, closing it firmly behind him. He placed his hat on her dresser.

She dropped to the bed. "It was a depressing supper," she said, meeting his eyes. "We're all so upset."

"Where's Dan?" He sat beside her.

"He's back in Dallas already. He wants to be in the office first thing in the morning. He's furious," she said. "I wish I could be madder, but I'm just upset. Really upset."

He pulled her tighter, nuzzling her neck. "It's not the end of the world, sweetheart. Of course you're upset. But it's not like you're horribly sick or—"

"It's the death of my job," she said softly.

He sighed. "Yes, it is." He stroked her hair. "Let's think about something else." He kissed her.

His kiss left her sizzling. As his lips left hers and touched her cheek, her forehead, her ear, and his breath caressed her neck, she leaned into him, electrified.

"RaeAnne," he murmured.

Inside, she felt warmth suffuse her body, replacing the icy feeling that had wedged inside her most of the day. They slid together so they were lying on the bed. Their tongues danced as he kissed her deeply.

"RaeAnne." His hand slipped under her T-shirt and cupped her breast, sending waves of longing through her, down to her very core. Then his lips replaced his fingers and he tugged her nipple. His sucking her through the flimsy material of her bra was incredibly erotic, and she arched toward him, rubbing against his body.

"Tyler…" she murmured, kissing him passionately.

Their tongues tangled, and she tasted coffee on his.

And then he was on top of her, pulling off her T-shirt and her bra, sucking her nipple.

Searing heat crashed through her like a wave. She grasped his shirt, pulling it off of him. His bare chest crushed hers, and it felt so freakin' good.

He pulled her jeans down. She was barefoot already so once he'd removed her jeans she wore only her lacy pink panties.

"God, you are gorgeous." He cupped her just where she wanted him to, and she thrust her body toward his hand. He stroked, then slipped off her panties.

"Tyler—please…" She moaned, barely able to think, wanting only to feel him inside of her. A want that burned like nothing she'd ever felt for anyone else.

He shucked his own jeans and boxers, and she heard the tear of foil. She stroked him.

"God, that feels so good. You're driving me crazy." He kissed her again and parted her thighs.

"Please," she panted.

He thrust into her, and she felt so good, so complete, that she wanted to yell out in pleasure. Something in her brain reminded her there were other people in nearby rooms, so she clamped down on her shout and merely gasped, "Oh, yes, yes…" as he rocked them both.

He slid out, then in again, each time bringing her closer to the edge.

He kissed her feverishly, kneading her breasts as he thrust.

And suddenly she went flying, into the galaxy.

"Tyler!" she gasped.

He moaned into her mouth and she felt him throb as he reached his peak inside her.

Slowly, slowly, they floated back to earth.

"RaeAnne," he said, kissing her slowly and ardently. "You feel so good. *This* feels so good."

"Hmmm," was all she could manage to murmur. "Yes."

They lay quietly together, locked in each other's arms. Slowly, RaeAnne became aware of their

131

surroundings. The faint music from down the hall. The smell of Tyler's aftershave, that blend of woodsy and leather. The hum of the air-conditioner, the cool air now touching her hot skin.

She felt *so* good. It was incredible.

"RaeAnne…" Tyler hugged her. "You don't have to go back to Dallas. Stay here."

His words wove around her muddled thoughts. "What?"

"Don't go back to Dallas. Stay in the canyon."

This time, his words sliced through her mental fog.

CHAPTER XI

She sat up, staring at him.

He opened his eyes and smiled.

"Stay in the canyon," he repeated, his voice entreating.

"Stay here?"

"Yes. Stay in the canyon, and we can be together. You can work on your book. You'll have time to finish it, now that you're not working for the magazine," he concluded. "And you can look around for something local—maybe one of the newspapers around here."

Shock barreled through her. Stay in the canyon? *Stay here with Tyler?*

"Are you kidding?" she gasped.

"Not at all." He sat up, too, and cupped her face. "You can stay here, work on your book, and be with me. It's the perfect solution."

"The perfect—Tyler, we hardly know each other," she protested.

The initial surprise of his suggestion was wearing off.

And it was being replaced by a surge of excitement and delight. A little voice inside her head was yelling "Yes! Yes!" as if through a megaphone.

The thought was tempting.

"I—I—" she stuttered.

She liked Tyler. She enjoyed spending time with him. The sex with him was nothing short of spectacular.

But staying on at the canyon? Possibly living with him?

But as her thoughts began to come together like the scattered pieces of a puzzle, she was struck by one.

It pierced her like an icicle falling through a snowbank on a cold Texas night.

The last thing she wanted to do was get involved with a hot cowboy. Sure, Tyler was a nice guy. He was being considerate right now. But, eventually, he could get bored, or find someone else. He'd walk away, like Ben.

And most of all, how could she trust her own feelings? Her own judgment?

And before he left her with a broken heart—she would nip this whole idea in the bud.

"I can't," she said.

"You can't?" He looked at her blankly. "Why not?"

"I just can't."

He tightened his hold on her. "If you doubt my feelings, don't," he whispered persuasively. "I'm in love with you, RaeAnne."

At his words, she felt a burst of happiness.

Quickly followed by a rush of fear.

Longing, and fright, bombarded her, tangling her insides into one gigantic knot. She wanted him to love her. She did.

But—she was afraid.

She stared at him. "You love me?"

"Yes," he replied, his eyes on her. "I do."

Oh, God, she *wanted to believe him.* And that in itself was terrifying.

She could not trust another cowboy, or believe in him.

Worst of all, she couldn't trust herself.

* * *

Tyler stared at RaeAnne. He'd just laid his heart on the line.

And she'd shoved it back in his face.

"RaeAnne," he said, his voice raspy. "I do love you."

"How can you?" She was staring at him as if he's grown another head. "You barely know me."

"I know enough." He reached for her.

She scooted to the other side of the bed. "No, you really don't. I care for you, Tyler. You're sweet and thoughtful and sex with you is unbelievable. More than I ever dreamed. But I feel like we barely know each other." Her expression revealed pain, and something else. Was she unsure of her feelings?

"You can get to know me over the next few weeks."

She shook her head, and now she did look sad, rather than disturbed. "I have to go back home. I have to find another job. I don't know how I feel about you."

"I know how I feel." He placed a hand on her shoulder. She was trembling. "I'm in love. I know exactly how I feel." The more he said it, the more he felt the truth of his words.

135

She stared at him, and he could swear he saw tears in her eyes.

"And I think you could be in love, too," he continued. He'd seen the way she reacted to him, her smiles when they spent time together, her happiness, the way she reacted when they made love. It wasn't just sex.

"Our—" He waved a hand and repeated his thought. "Our love-making isn't just about sex. "

"Why do you say that?" Her voice was shaky.

"Your reaction. The way you kiss me, the way you respond." He stroked her cheek. "I think you *do* love me." He was taking a chance saying that, but he hoped she did. Suspected she did. But for some reason, she was afraid.

She sighed. "I do have feelings for you, but even if I did think I was in love…"

"Even if you did think you were in love… ?" he echoed.

"How can I be sure? I mean—" She stopped, and her face showed confusion and uncertainty.

"What is it?" he asked, more gently. Something was making her hesitant, keeping her from throwing herself into his arms as he'd expected she would.

She shook her head. "I just don't know."

Shock reverberated through him. It wasn't *him* she doubted, was uncertain of; she doubted herself.

"RaeAnne," he said. "You don't trust yourself, do you?"

"How can I?" Her tone was bitter. "Look at my history, my mother. She made plenty of mistakes with men. How do I know I won't do the same? How can I be sure I'm a fit judge of a man's character? I sure wasn't with Ben." She sucked in a breath.

"RaeAnne?" He reached for her again.

She slid out of bed.

"I may not be able to convince you that you are a good judge of character," he said hoarsely. "But I sure as hell can tell you I'm not going anywhere. I'm in love with you."

She grabbed a blue robe from the desk chair. She pulled it on, her shoulders sagging.

"I'm sorry," she whispered. "I just can't believe that. It's too soon. Maybe if I'd met you another time, or in another place…" Her words drifted off.

He got out of bed, and walked over to where she stood, her body radiating dejection. "This is a time to be happy," he said. "You have a guy who adores you. Me." He felt his stomach knotting.

She swiveled around, biting her lip as he watched.

"You really don't believe me," he said, hurt and disbelief warring inside him. "You really don't believe you have good judgement."

"No." It came out almost as a groan.

"RaeAnne—" he implored.

But she shook her head. "No, Tyler. It's impossible. You better go."

He'd just laid his heart on the line, and she was ordering him to *leave*? This was ridiculous. Anger began to simmer in his gut.

"You're not giving me a chance. We're so good together—"

"Maybe now, but how do we know what will happen in a few weeks or months?" she challenged. "Can't you see? I can't take the chance."

And that, he thought, was the gist of it. She was

afraid to risk her heart. Afraid she would get hurt again.

He reached out again, but she moved away.

Her old boyfriend had just appeared here a few days ago. That had to be what her fear was about.

"I'm not like your old boyfriend," he protested hotly. "Don't compare me to him. I'm nicer, kinder—and I obviously care a lot more. Don't compare me to some jerk." His tone became disgusted. "If you can't see how much I care--"

A tear rolled down her cheek.

"Well," he said, "there's nothing I can do if you won't believe me." He turned around and gathered his clothes.

"I wish I could," she blurted.

He slid on his boxers, then his jeans. "You could if you wanted to." The anger was still simmering inside his gut.

"It's not that simple."

He sat down and pulled on his boots. "It could be."

"I wish it could be." Her voice was so low he barely heard her.

He grabbed his T-shirt. "It could be, if you want it to," he said again. Pulling his T-shirt over his head, he ran his hand though his hair. Then he picked up his Stetson and shoved it onto his head. The lava-like heat of anger bubbled up, threatening to overflow. Before he could say something he'd regret, he headed toward the door.

She sidestepped away.

Even that action was a knife to his gut.

"When you realize how much I care, and you're ready to move forward," he said, his voice low, "call me."

He opened the door and walked out, anger and hurt warring inside him. He wanted to punch the wall.

He wanted to cry.

But even more, he wanted to kiss her again.

* * *

She hardly slept that night.

RaeAnne dragged herself to breakfast, exhausted. She loaded up on coffee and ate with Sean, who was almost finished with his meal. Kristy joined them a few minutes later, looking as pale as RaeAnne knew she must.

She'd finished packing except for her toiletries last night, crying after Tyler left. She suspected she was in love with him, too. But how could she trust her judgment about what kind of man he was? She'd been wrong before. Just like her mother.

By nine AM, she and Kristy were right behind Sean on their way back to Dallas.

The trip was sad. Kristy asked a few questions about Tyler, but RaeAnne cut her off, saying she wasn't sure they were going to keep seeing each other.

"Really? You two seemed to be crazy about each other."

RaeAnne shrugged, and switched on the radio.

The man singing about how some woman had broken his heart didn't help her mood.

They went directly to the *Texas Trails'* office. There, they met with a woman from Human Resources of the new company who outlined their severance packages. To RaeAnne's relief, she'd have her salary for several months, which meant she wouldn't have to worry about making ends meet for a little while.

Still, she'd be cautious financially, in case it took time to find a job.

Packing up her desk, her photos, and personal effects wasn't fun either. She waited for Kristy to finish and offered her a ride home. The two of them were mostly silent as she drove, and agreed to meet for dinner the following week.

"It's the end of an era," Kristy said sadly as she exited the car.

RaeAnne got home, lugged in her suitcase, duffle bag, laptop, and the box of stuff from her job.

Her apartment was quiet. She dropped everything near the front door, too fatigued to unpack. Too late, she remembered she had little food in the house since she hadn't expected to be back until the weekend. Well, she was just too tired to drag herself to the grocery store now. It could wait for tomorrow.

She and Kristy hadn't had lunch, so she was getting hungry. She had some cheese and crackers, then showered, and got into her most comfortable summer pajamas despite the fact that it was barely four o'clock in the afternoon. She could order a pizza.

She also had some whiskey in her apartment. It would come in handy tonight., she suspected.

Then she sat in her big chair, and cried.

* * *

Two weeks later, RaeAnne got off the bus and walked the four blocks to her apartment complex late in the afternoon.

The day was warm with clouds crowding the sky, but the sun wasn't beating down on her as she walked.

140

It had been an interesting and hopeful afternoon. She'd had a long interview at *Down Home Texas Bride* magazine. She liked the people she'd met but knew the competition to be an assistant editor at the popular publication was going to be fierce.

As she walked, holding her tote with samples of some of her work, the thought occurred to her that she would enjoy doing freelance articles for the magazine. Even if she worked for another company, she could certainly try to do that, since not all their articles were produced in-house. As long as she didn't work for a competing magazine, that might be another option.

Of course, it might hurt working on bridal, happily-ever-after pieces.

Not if you were living with Tyler, maybe engaged, and working totally freelance, that voice in her head piped up to declare.

She sighed.

She missed Tyler. Missed his voice, his smiles, and his hands stroking her…

She would not go there.

He'd never said anything about marriage. Only about her living in the canyon, working on her book, spending time with him—

The funny thing was, she was thinking of the canyon frequently, too.

She sighed as images of Tyler's handsome face, his hunky body, his engaging smile bombarded her. Heat from remembered embraces surrounded her.

She longed for him so much it was almost physical.

She opened her door, shut it behind her, then walked to the wall where she turned the air-conditioner thermostat down several degrees.

141

She collapsed into her favorite chair.

Yeah, she missed Tyler. Terribly.

And the fact that she also missed Palo Duro canyon was a surprise. The wildflowers, the strong wind that sometimes broke up the solid wall of heat, the animals—horses, dogs, cats.

The people.

Ah, the residents of the canyon were so different from the people of Dallas, where everyone rushed around, intent on getting somewhere, absorbed by their own business.

The people of Palo Duro canyon greeted each other. Really wanted to know how you were doing, who you were related to, what kinds of things you enjoyed.

She wasn't used to that homey feel, that comfort of really knowing your neighbors. Here, she barely knew the couple who lived upstairs from her, or the man next door whose kid visited him every weekend. She had only spoken to the two elderly sisters upstairs from him a couple of times.

She glanced at the clock. Almost four-thirty. She'd be meeting her sister, who was on summer break from the school where she taught fourth grade, for dinner tomorrow evening. MaryBeth had just returned from a trip to the Bahamas with friends, and wanted to tell her all about it.

MaryBeth had also probed about her business trip to the canyon, and she'd reluctantly promised to tell her about that when they met.

She kicked off her nice shoes and went to wash up, and, afterward, sat at her computer, searching, again, for a job.

Dan had been lucky. He'd landed at a prestigious ranching magazine almost straightaway. Those photos of his from The Golden Q had to have helped him get that job, and at a better salary than what he'd been making at *Texas Trails*.

Kristy and Sean were still looking, although both, like RaeAnne, had been on a couple of interviews.

After half an hour, she checked her email, then social media.

The ringing of her doorbell startled her.

Glancing at her watch, she saw it was after 5. Who could be at her door? Maybe one of the neighbors?

She peeked through the peephole and reeled back.

Ben. What the hell was he doing here?

"Please, I need to speak with you," he said.

"Why?" she demanded through the closed door.

"I just found out about your magazine. Please let me in," he implored.

She hesitated, then grabbed her cell phone and keys, and walked out to meet him, her stomach clenched.

"We can talk out here." She shut the door behind her. She did *not* want him inside her apartment. If he was whining and begging, she was afraid she'd have trouble getting rid of him.

"I heard about *Texas Trails* being sold today," he began. He stepped forward, but she sidestepped, keeping him a few yards away.

"You're going to need a job," he said, giving her a smile. "And probably some help to tide you over." His expression looked decidedly smug to her. His grin grated on her nerves. "This would be a good time to turn to me."

Arrogant asshole! She gritted her teeth. "It would?"

He seemed unaware of the sarcasm edging her voice.

"Yes," he replied, his grin growing wider.

"So you think now that I'm down on my luck you can waltz back into my life? After you dumped me?"

"Well—ugh—"He looked surprised. "I didn't — exactly—dump you. You found—well, let's not talk about that." He swept his hand through his hair. "And a couple of weeks ago, you weren't exactly the most friendly girlfriend."

"Yes you did break up with me," she interrupted. The knot in her stomach unwound. She smirked. "Why would I want to go back to you after the way you treated me last year?"

"Because I care." He was no longer smiling.

So does someone else, she thought. *So does Tyler.*

And she knew, with searing clarity, that it was true.

Tyler cared. He loved her. Not in the way Ben had professed to; Tyler didn't look down at her, nor was he condescending. No, Tyler cared about her as a person, not for what she could do for him or how he could show her off. And she'd bet her last dollar he wouldn't cheat.

She mentally shoved Ben away as she stared at him with narrowed eyes.

"Get lost, Ben," she declared. "I don't need you."

"Yes, you do—"

"No," she retorted. "I don't." She spun around and headed to her door. When she reached it, she glanced at him. "We're finished."

"RaeAnne—" he whined.

"Goodbye, Ben," she said. "We're done." She said it firmly so he wouldn't argue. Then she opened the door, walked inside, shut it, and locked the deadbolt.

She marched into her kitchen, not waiting to see him leave. She took ice water out of the fridge and gulped some down.

There was silence outside. She hoped he'd leave and not try to change her mind.

Ben hadn't changed. He was still concerned with himself. Still condescending.

She heard a car start.

She peeked out her bedroom window, to see a fancy red sports car leaving the parking lot. She heard the squeal of tires as he pulled out into the street.

Sagging against the wall, she let out a breath of relief.

That was that! He was out of her life.

Now... what was she going to do about Tyler? She had conflicting feelings—and she wanted to discuss them with her sister.

* * *

As soon as her sister got to her apartment, RaeAnne told her she wanted her advice.

She began by showing MaryBeth some of the photos of the canyon that Kristy had printed and given RaeAnne.

"These really are great," her sister said, studying several. "And you said these—" she pointed to four RaeAnne had put to one side—"are from the location of episodes of *The Cattle Drive*?"

"Yes," RaeAnne answered.

MaryBeth got up and walked over to the digital frame that stood on one of RaeAnne's bookcases. Picking it up, she returned to the couch where they were sitting and placed it on the coffee table with the other photos which were printed out. The digital frame had been off, but now she flicked it on with the touch of her finger.

Dusk was falling, and RaeAnne had lit a soothing vanilla candle whose fragrance permeated the air. She took a deep breath. She usually left this device off since she knew there were several photos of Ben and her on it.

The first photos that popped up were of her and MaryBeth taken during the last few years, at a county fair, at Thanksgiving, and one at a party MaryBeth had hosted.

The images scrolled. There were a few of her and Tara, then one of her and Kristy on a photo shoot they'd done in April.

And several with Ben. Ben with his arm around her at a party. Ben with his cousin's daughter and her at his cousin's wedding. Ben and her on Halloween in Victorian-era clothing.

RaeAnne reached out and turned it off. "I have to delete those photos of Ben." Rapidly, she filled her sister in on what happened at Palo Duro canyon, her romance with Tyler, their argument, and Ben's visit there, and his visit again yesterday.

"Is this Tyler?" MaryBeth pointed to his handsome face in one of Kristy's photos.

"Yes." RaeAnne sighed. "MaryBeth, I'm in love with him. But—I'm scared."

"Why?" Her sister's brows knitted.

"Just, look at our history! I'm like Mom. A poor judge of character."

"What do you mean?" her sister questioned.

She sighed again. "Look, Mom has gone from one guy to the next since Dad passed. A drunk, a cheater—she isn't a good judge of character. And I'm the same," she added, sadly.

"I don't think so," her sister objected.

"It's true. Look how wrong I was about Ben."

MaryBeth shook her head. "Originally, maybe. You were younger and less experienced. But not now. You sent him packing last night."

"Yes," RaeAnne agreed. "But what does that prove?"

"It proves you judged him well last night. That he was a crawling snake who showed up here because he figured you were in a bad situation, and he intended to take advantage of that and get you back. You trusted your gut and told him no." She regarded RaeAnne.

Something shimmied up RaeAnne's spine. Hope.

"But—but that doesn't mean I'm a good judge of character," she said.

"No? What about Kristy?"

"What about her?" RaeAnne asked.

MaryBeth smiled. "When she applied for that job at *Texas Trails*, you championed her and took her under your wing when she was hired. You knew she'd been an alcoholic."

"Yes…" RaeAnne was starting to see what MaryBeth was getting at. She gripped her fingers together.

"You judged her to be a good person, someone who

147

had left drinking behind, and was sober," MaryBeth said. "You made a good judgment call there."

It was as if a lightbulb snapped on inside of her. RaeAnne almost gasped out loud.

She had gone with her gut, and knew that Kristy would turn out to be dependable. She had trusted her judgment.

And she'd been right!

"See?" MaryBeth must have recognized the wheels turning in her mind. She smiled widely.

"I'm not like our mother!" RaeAnne exclaimed.

"Stop comparing yourself to her. You're a much better judge of character."

For the first time in days, RaeAnne smiled. A large, happy smile.

"That's my sis," MaryBeth said, leaning back on the couch.

"I'm a better judge of character," RaeAnne repeated.

"Absolutely."

"So I can depend on my judgment of Tyler," RaeAnne concluded, her voice dropping to a whisper.

"Yup."

"He is special. The most wonderful man I've ever met."

"And you can take that to the bank," MaryBeth finished with a laugh.

RaeAnne stood up and whirled around, then pulled her sister into a gigantic hug. "Thank you! Thank—"Her heart fell. "But I broke it off." Her voice cracked.

"So what are you going to do about it?" MaryBeth challenged.

RaeAnne stuck her chin up. "I'm going to win him back."

CHAPTER XI

On Friday, RaeAnne stood in the shadowy barn, waiting.

She'd enlisted Clay and Missy's help. Clay had asked Tyler to take his truck to pick up more fencing, so RaeAnne could arrive while he wasn't around. Once she had, Clay had saddled Thunder.

She inhaled, her heart beating a mile a minute. She couldn't remember ever feeling like this. So much depended on her plan going right—and on Tyler's reaction.

She took a deep breath and smelled horses, leather, and fresh hay. A horse nearby snuffled, and one of the cats near her feet yawned. Sweat trickled down her neck and she wiped it away with her hand.

Reaching for her water bottle, she took a gulp of the cool liquid. As she put it aside, she heard the crunch of tires on the graveled parking area.

He was here.

She swallowed. His truck door slammed and she heard the sound of his boots.

"Clay, is that RaeAnne's car?" Tyler shouted to his brother.

That was her cue. She stepped outside into the sunlight, leading Thunder.

"RaeAnne?" Tyler asked.

His hair was tousled and there were shadows under his eyes. But despite them, he looked wonderful.

"Hi, Tyler," she said, a lilt in her voice. She prayed he would be happy to see her!

He looked wary.

"Will you come for a ride with me? Like we did that first day of the photo shoot?"

"You want to ride with me on Thunder?" His mouth fell open.

"Yes." She took a deep breath. "Please?"

"Sure."

Relief coursed through her as he boosted her up, then swung onto the horse. His familiar, woodsy scent greeted her.

Instead of sitting stiffly like she had that first time, she moved her butt on the blanket to sit closer to Tyler, and leaned back against him. He sucked in a breath. She could feel his heat through her T-shirt.

"Tyler." She was serious now, as she regarded him over her shoulder. "The first time I sat with you like this for the photos—do you know what I thought?'

He shook his head. "No."

"I thought that you were just another hot cowboy, and—"

"You thought I was hot?" He raised his eyebrows.

"Absolutely," she responded. "And, I thought.... that I was stuck in the saddle with you."

"Yeah?"

"Yes. But now—I want to be with you, Tyler. Always." She finished, watching him anxiously.

For a moment longer, he stared. Then the corners of his mouth lifted. "Always?" he echoed.

"Always." She twisted in front of him, reaching up to wrap her arms around his neck and pull his head down until their mouths met.

She kissed him, hard, and he responded with the most searing kiss she'd ever felt in her life. Electricity sizzled to her toes.

She pulled back slightly. "Yes," she murmured, gazing up into his eyes, and knew her own were damp. "I love you, Tyler. I couldn't stop thinking about you but I doubted myself. Doubted you. And now I know for certain. We have something special. I *want* to be stuck with you. Right here in the canyon."

His smile was dazzling, and happiness shot through her as she gazed at him and realized how happy he was, too.

"You've changed," he said hoarsely. "You've accepted our love." He practically jumped off Thunder, then grabbed her by the waist and lifted her down, until her body slid against his. Then, he kissed her hard and furiously.

Her heart beat so rapidly she thought it would erupt from her chest.

Finally he let her go. His eyes were gleaming as they searched her face.

"I do love you," she whispered.

"Clay?" he called, and she saw his brother approaching, grinning widely and clapping. "Can you take care of Thunder for me?"

"Sure," his brother answered, his tone jovial.

One arm still surrounding her, Tyler caressed her cheek. "We have plans to make," he said softly. "Let's go back to my place and make them."

"Yes," she answered breathlessly. "I like your

151

Roni Denholtz

idea. I can stay in the canyon, work on my book, and we can make love every night."

"I want more," he declared.

"More?"

"I want always and forever, too." He clasped her hands, then dropped to one knee. "RaeAnne Tilton, will you do me the very great honor of marrying me, darlin'?"

Her heart in her throat, she gazed down at his beloved face. "Yes," she whispered. And then, louder, "Oh yes!"

With a whoop, he pulled her into his arms and whirled her around.

"I love you, RaeAnne," he said when he set her on the ground. "Always will."

"Me, too," she answered.

Applause and whistles burst out around them, and RaeAnne looked to see Clay and a bunch of the cowhands clapping as they surrounded them.

"Meet the future Mrs. Quimby," Tyler boasted.

She flushed with pleasure as he took her hand in a firm grip. Looking up at him, she smiled.

"We'll be happily-ever-after stuck in the saddle together," she said.

He bent to kiss her. "We sure will."

THE END

ABOUT THE AUTHOR

Roni Denholtz has published 8 novels and one novella. Her books have been nominated for the New Jersey Golden Leaf Award and the National Readers' Choice Award. "Marquis in a Minute" won the NJ Golden Leaf award for Best Regency Romance. She has also written dozens of short stories and articles for magazines such as "Baby Talk," "Child Life," and "For the Bride." She is the author of 9 children's books, published by January Productions. "Jenny Gets Glasses" was named #7 of the Top Twenty Favorite Books of First Graders in a nationwide study by the Reading is Fundamental Group.

A former special education teacher, Roni also taught "Writing for Fun and Profit" in her local adult school for many years and some of her students went on to get published.

Roni is a member of New Jersey Romance Writers, where she served as president for the 2016 year; Romance Writers of America; and the Authors Guild. When her children were younger, she also was active in Marching Band Parents, Robotics Parents, and PTA.

Roni and her husband own an independent real estate company, Jersey Success Realty, in northwestern New Jersey. They have two grown children and a rescue dog. Roni served on the board of Noah's Ark Animal Shelter for 8 years..

She is an avid reader, and enjoys photography, cooking and travel.

She loves to hear from readers! Find her on facebook and on her webpage at www.ronidenholtz.com

Made in the USA
Middletown, DE
25 May 2017